To Kyle

Always and forever

1

★ Big Dreams ★

From the time she was old enough to hold her first pair of scissors in kindergarten, Mickey Williams knew she wanted to be a fashion designer. Way before she could even read, she and her mom pored over issues of *Vogue*, *Elle*, and *InStyle* together, tearing out pages of their favorite couture looks. Not many little girls knew who Coco Chanel was, but Mickey considered the fashion icon her idol and inspiration—not to mention Donatella Versace, Miuccia Prada, and Stella McCartney.

"What do you think?" she asked her mom. It was her sixth birthday, and she was giving one of her presents—Pink and Pretty Barbie—an extreme makeover.

She held up the doll that she'd wrapped head to toe in tinfoil and stickers. She'd braided its hair into an intricate updo and topped it off with a red-pen cap.

Her mom studied the outfit. She was always one hundred percent honest with her.

"I think it's a bit avant-garde," her mom replied. "A little edgy for Barbie. But that said…I like it. It's very Alexander McQueen."

Mickey nodded. "I was trying to dress her for a runway show in outer space."

"Aha," her mom replied thoughtfully. "Then I'd say that look fits the bill."

Mickey smiled. Her friends in first grade all thought she was crazy for chopping off her dolls' hair and coloring it with neon-green highlighter markers. They were grossed out when she replaced each doll's elegant evening gown with scraps of old clothing. But who wanted her Barbie to look like a clone of thousands of others on the toy store shelf? Mickey wanted all her dolls to be individuals in one-of-a-kind outfits. She could always find tons of fabric scraps at the Sunday flea market—all sorts of velvets, satins, plaids, and brocades in every color of the rainbow. For five dollars, she could take home a whole bag full! She and her mom loved hunting for treasures among the rows of cluttered booths.

"Do you like this?" her mom asked one Sunday as

they roamed through the stalls of treasures. She held up a brooch shaped like a peacock that was missing a few blue stones and attached it to the lapel of her denim jacket. "If you don't get too close, you don't even notice."

Mickey examined the pin with a critical eye. It made her mom's blue eyes pop, but it was kind of old-fashioned looking—what *Vogue* would call "so yesterday."

"Pass," she said, and picked up another pin—this one a dazzling emerald-green clover made of Swarovski crystals. "This looks so pretty with your red hair. And four-leaf clovers are lucky." It was only five dollars—a steal!

"I love it," her mom said, turning to the vendor. She hugged Mickey. "What would I do without you, Mickey Mouse?"

But Mickey's classmates were not quite as appreciative of her talents. In second grade, when she offered to give her friend Ally's doll a makeover, she never expected the little girl to burst into tears.

"You ruined my princess!" she wailed on a playdate. "I'm telling!"

Mickey examined her handiwork: Cinderella clearly needed a new look, so she'd given it to her. She combed her long blond hair out of its updo and gave it a swingy shoulder-length cut that resembled hers. Then she high-lighted it with an orange marker. Finally, she taped on a black felt miniskirt and a red, plaid strapless top.

"I think she looks pretty," she said, trying to stop Ally's bawling. "She could be on a magazine cover now."

Ally wasn't buying it. "I want my mommy!" she screamed, until Mickey's mom came running in and calmed her down with the promise of a glass of chocolate milk.

"Mickey, seriously?" her mom whispered to her. "Now I'm going to have to go buy Ally a new Cinderella doll—and I barely have enough money to pay the rent this month!"

Mickey felt awful. She knew how hard her mom worked behind the makeup counter at Wanamaker's Department Store—sometimes seven days a week, from opening till closing.

"I'll pay for it," Mickey promised her. "I have money saved up in my piggy bank that Aunt Olive gave me for my birthday."

Her mom shook her head. "Honey, I know you were just playing, but you have to use your head." She ruffled Mickey's blond curls. "If something doesn't belong to you, please don't give it a fashion makeover."

It wasn't the first time and it wouldn't be the last time

that Mickey got in trouble for "redesigning." In fourth-grade home ec class, the assignment was to sew a simple skirt to wear for the school's spring festival. Most girls chose a pretty pastel fabric: pink, baby blue, or lavender in tiny floral prints. Mickey's skirt was…different.

"Oh my!" Ms. Farrell gasped when Mickey walked into the classroom modeling it. She'd found a shiny brown python pleather and trimmed it with perfect tiny green stitches around the hemline.

"Is it supposed to be a witch's costume?" Ally asked.

"No, it's supposed to be Mother Nature," Mickey insisted. "It's earthy."

Ms. Farrell didn't know what to say. "It's…very… unique," she stammered. "Maybe we can put it up on display, and you can make another skirt that's less, well, dramatic."

But Mickey was determined. "No, I'm wearing the skirt I made. I'm not going to make one that looks like everyone else's."

So when they stood on the auditorium stage and sang, "A Tisket, A Tasket, I Made a May Basket," she stuck out like a sore thumb. It wasn't that she wanted to. It was simply that she had to be herself.

Her art teacher Mrs. Archer was one of the few people who actually "got" her. Her BFF Annabelle tried—they'd lived in the same apartment building in Philadelphia since they were toddlers—but she didn't quite understand why Mickey was so driven. Or why fashion rules were meant to be broken.

In the middle of fifth grade, her teacher handed her a brochure for the Fashion Academy of Brooklyn (FAB for short). "Have you heard of it?" Mrs. Archer asked her.

Mickey had not just heard of it, she'd dreamed about it. It was simply *the* best middle school in the country for kids who wanted to become fashion designers.

"I know it's in New York, but I also know how much fashion design means to you," Mrs. Archer told her. "Maybe if you talk it over with your mom?"

Mickey knew better than to open that can of worms. There was no way her mom would agree to sending her to FAB, unless...

She filled out the application and checked the box requesting a scholarship. Then she attached copies of her designs and snapped pictures of Annabelle modeling them.

"Try and look fierce," she instructed her bestie. "Put your hand on your hip, look deeply into the camera, and tilt your head to the side." She tucked a stray strand of Annabelle's long, wavy, dark-brown hair behind her ear. "Could you try and not look so awkward?"

"I feel ridiculous," Annabelle replied, trying to balance the hat Mickey had designed—a lopsided saucer—and still keep her stare from wavering. "And my skirt is pinching."

Mickey made a few adjustments to the black pleather mini and made sure that the gray tweed moto jacket sat perfectly on her friend's shoulders. "Fit is everything," she explained. "Tailoring can make or break a design."

"Uh-huh," Annabelle said, stifling a yawn. "Mick, we've been at this for hours. How many more outfits do I have to put on?"

When Mickey was done shooting four more looks, she placed all the materials in the envelope and scribbled her mom's name at the bottom of the application. The following day, she handed it back to her teacher to mail.

"Oh! I'm so glad your mother decided to let you try out!" Mrs. Archer said.

"Well, she said I could give it a shot," Mickey lied. "I mean, the chances are pretty slim, right?"

And that was that. She practically forgot about FAB, until a large, white envelope arrived in the mail four months later, shortly before elementary school graduation.

"What is this?" her mom asked, examining it.

Mickey snatched it out of her hand and tore into the envelope. Inside was a course catalog, a financial aid package, and a letter that read, "Congratulations! Welcome to FAB!"

"No way!" Mickey screamed. "I don't believe it!"

Her mom read over her shoulder. "Neither do I. Mickey, what did you do?"

She was too excited to cover her tracks. "I mailed in the application. I kinda signed your name and told my teacher you were cool with it. Mom, do you realize what this means?"

"Yes. That my daughter forged my name and lied to her teacher and to her mother. Mackenzie Elizabeth Williams, I thought we never lied to each other."

"This wasn't a lie—because I didn't know they would give me a scholarship. It was kind of a wish that I wasn't planning to mention unless it came true."

Her mother shook her head. "Mickey, we can't just up and move to New York," she said. "Even if I could get another job there, we don't have a place to live or money to afford an apartment in the city. I can barely pay our rent now, and New York is twice as expensive."

"I know—which is why I was hoping you'd call Aunt Olive and ask her if I could come stay with her?"

That last suggestion pushed her mom over the edge. She was now pacing the floor, waving her hands in the air, and yelling. "Olive? You want me to call my sister—whom I barely speak to—and ask her if she'll take you in for the next three years? And you want me to send my only daughter to live three hundred miles away?"

Mickey nodded. "In a nutshell—yes."

"This is ridiculous. You're going to write a very nice letter to the admissions people at FAB and say thanks but no thanks."

Mickey felt her heart sink. "Mom, I know it's a long way away from Philly, but it's all I've ever wanted."

"You can still be a fashion designer when you grow up," her mother insisted, "without picking up and moving to a strange city."

"It's not strange. It's New York. I love New York!" Mickey replied.

"You love going ice-skating at Rockefeller Center at Christmas and shopping for fabric in the garment district," her mom said. "You don't have any idea what it's like to live there. Besides, all your friends are here. *I'm* here."

Her mom suddenly got quiet, and Mickey sensed that was what this argument was all about. Ten years ago, when she was just a baby, her dad had left as well. All she and her mom had was each other.

"I'll come home on the train on weekends," Mickey promised. "And I'll Skype every night. It'll be like I never left. Mrs. Archer says they only take 'the crème de la crème' of design students. I can't say no!"

"Let me think about it," her mom said, sighing. "And let me speak to Aunt Olive." She made a face. "That should be fun…"

Mickey hugged her. "You're the best mom in the whole world."

"Or the biggest pushover," her mom grumbled. "I'm not saying yes. I'm saying I'll think about it."

Big Apple Bound

It took three more days to convince her mom—and another week of her mom pleading with Aunt Olive—but they both finally gave in. Mickey double pinkie-sweared her mother that she'd be careful, get nothing less than Bs in all her classes, and never talk to strangers on the subway.

"You've never been away from home," her mom reminded her. "Are you sure you're going to be okay with this?"

"It's like sleepaway camp," Mickey tried to rationalize. "Annabelle's been going all the way to Vermont every summer since she was eight. If she can handle it, I can." Camp had never been a possibility since her mom couldn't afford it. But with FAB offering her a full scholarship, there were no excuses.

"What if you have a nightmare? Who'll bring you warm milk and rub your back? Certainly not your aunt Olive!"

"I'll be fine, Jordana," she said. Her mom let her call her by her first name whenever she wanted to sound mature and grown up. Mickey wasn't about to admit that the idea of being away from her mom every night made her a little anxious. She would put on a brave face and simply spend as much time with her mother over the summer as she could.

She hung out at Wanamaker's during the days watching her work her makeup magic. "I have my daughter's law school graduation this weekend, Jordana," her steady customer Mrs. Gates filled her in. "Do you think we could do a smoky eye? Get rid of the wrinkles?"

Mickey's mom studied her face from every angle. She held a slanted brush between her teeth and didn't dare dip it into a pot of shadow until she knew her exact plan of attack.

"I would do a warm brown-and-bronze eye," she said, nodding. "Yes, definitely brown, not gray. And a contoured cheek with a very pale lip. Maybe a frosty nude—no, an icy pink." Mickey giggled. It was as if her mother were a doctor prescribing medicine.

"Oh! You are a genius!" the woman cooed. "Truly, a makeup genius."

Mickey felt the same way—her mother definitely had an artistic gift.

"Why didn't you ever go to New York City and work at Fashion Week? Or a photo shoot for a magazine?" Mickey asked her one night when they were setting up folding chairs on the roof to watch the sunset.

Her mom shrugged. "I guess I got comfy here," she said. "Sometimes comfy is okay, honey. You don't always have to go off gallivanting around the country to prove something."

Mickey knew she was referring to her father. Shortly after she was born, her dad decided he wanted to travel with his band and be a rock star. So he left one day and never came home again. Simple as that. In the past ten years she couldn't recall a single phone call or birthday card, and her mother never spoke his name. (For the record, it was Doug.) She knew how much it hurt her mom at the time, but Mickey could almost understand it—her dad's need for adventure, for excitement, for a life that was bigger and bolder than the one he had. He never did become a star (unless you counted a few singles that scraped on the bottom of the charts), but at least he gave it his best shot. Her mom said it was irresponsible, but Mickey couldn't blame him for wanting more or for seizing the chance when it presented itself. She was a lot like him that way.

The summer flew by, and middle school was staring her right in the face. She and Annabelle made plans to meet up at their fave froyo place the day she got home from camp.

"I don't get it," Annabelle said, thoughtfully licking a cone. "I mean, why would you want to go to a new school where you don't know anyone?"

"I want to be a designer," Mickey replied. "FAB is where you go to be a designer."

"Couldn't you just go to middle school in Philly here with me and still be a designer?" Annabelle pleaded. "We've been friends since first grade. It'll be totally weird without you."

Mickey knew Annabelle depended on her—not just for answers on their science homework and advice on what to wear—but for emotional support as well.

"I don't have any clue what I want to be when I grow up," her friend admitted. "How come you always know things?"

Mickey shrugged. "You'll figure it out. You're really good at dancing. Maybe you'll be a Rockette!"

Annabelle rolled her eyes. "Puh-lease. As if my parents would *ever* let me be a dancer! My mom's a lawyer and my dad's a radiologist. They're sending me to law school or medical school, like it or not."

Mickey knew that was probably true. Unlike her mom, who always encouraged her to follow her passion, Annabelle's parents put a lot of pressure on her to get straight As in school, take piano lessons, speak Latin…

"You're totally gonna forget I exist." Her friend interrupted her thoughts.

"No way!" Mickey replied. "How could I forget the person who broke my toe with her bike in first grade?"

Annabelle laughed. "That was an accident. Your toe got in the way of my wheel."

Mickey held up her flip-flop. "See? My pinkie toe is still crooked. All I have to do to remember you is look at it."

"Well, just in case you need reminding…" Annabelle handed her a small box with a ribbon on top.

"What's this?" Mickey asked. "It's not a going-away present, is it? 'Cause I'm not going away! I'll be home so much on the weekends and holidays you'll get sick of seeing me."

"Just open it," Annabelle said.

Mickey took off the lid and saw there was a small silver thimble charm on a chain.

"I couldn't find a sewing machine charm," Annabelle said softly. "This was the best I could do. I kinda think it says 'fashion designer,' don't you?"

Mickey threw her arms around her friend and hugged her tight. "It's the best present ever!" She took it out of the box and secured it around her neck. "I'll never take it off."

"Eww. Not even on Field Day? Because you get so disgustingly sweaty," Annabelle teased her.

"Okay, maybe on Field Day. But that's the only time."

They finished their cones and said a quick good-bye.

"I'll call you and let you know all about FAB," Mickey promised.

"I'll call you when I need help with my biology homework," Annabelle replied. "And you are so coming home to help me dissect a frog."

As she walked back down the street to her apartment, Mickey wanted desperately to look back and wave. But she knew if she did, it would be that much harder. So instead, she kept walking.

3

The Olliegator

"Here we are," Mickey's mom said when they arrived at Aunt Olive's three-story walk-up on West 88th and Columbus. They had somehow managed to get all of Mickey's luggage on the train from Philly to NYC, and now the cab driver was unloading it on the curb.

"Is that it?" the driver asked, mopping his brow. "What do you call this thing?" He set Mickey's dress form down on the sidewalk. "It's like a headless, armless, legless mannequin on wheels!" he said.

Mickey chuckled. "That's Edith," she explained to the puzzled man. "I named her after Edith Head, one of the most famous costume designers in fashion design history."

"Uh-huh," the man said, looking puzzled. "Where'd her head go?"

"Dress forms don't need a head," Mickey said. "You use them to fit your designs. Sometimes I sew right on her! I got Edith at a yard sale for fifteen dollars in the fourth grade. We've been inseparable ever since."

Her mom paid the fare, and the driver pulled off. "I suppose that you, Edith, and I should head on up to Aunt Olive's," she said.

They rang the buzzer for 3B and waited patiently for Olive to buzz her up.

"Aren't you coming in?" Mickey asked when her mom paused at the third-floor landing.

"It's probably better if I don't," her mother hesitated. "Olive and I don't exactly get along." She set Mickey's sewing machine down on the floor next to her. "I'm sure you'll do great, honey. But if you ever want to come home—even tomorrow—you can just change your mind. You know the door is wide open."

Mickey took a deep breath and rang the doorbell. Olive looked through the peephole and barked, "Who's there?"

Mickey's mom shook her head and shouted, "Who do you think it is, Olive? It's us!"

She gave Mickey one last hug. "See ya on the weekend, right?"

Mickey nodded. "It's only a week away, Mom. I'll see you Saturday. Every Saturday! I promise!"

She watched her mom descend the stairs then heard several locks and bolts turn on the other side of the door.

Aunt Olive poked her head out and glared at Mickey. "Are you going to just stand there or are you coming in?" she asked. "I see your mother was too rude to come in and greet me."

Mickey forced a smile and tried to be pleasant and friendly. "Hi, Aunt Olive!" she said. "I'm so happy to be here!" She went to hug her aunt, but instead Olive extended her hand. Mickey wasn't sure if she was supposed to shake it or kiss it!

She looked around the apartment: it was a small but tidy two-bedroom with several paintings of birds on the walls. In fact, as Olive gave her the tour, she realized there were birds everywhere: dozens of tiny porcelain ones, bird-decorated towels in the bathroom, even a real parakeet perched in a cage in the living room.

"Wow, you like birds, huh?" Mickey said, poking her finger through the bars at the fluffy, little, yellow creature chirping at her.

"Murray bites," Olive grunted. "Keep your fingers away."

"Oh!" Mickey replied. "Thanks for the tip."

"I am an ornithologist," Olive explained.

Mickey looked confused. "Is that like an eye doctor or something?"

Olive huffed. "No, it's a bird-watcher. If you want, you can tag along with me this weekend to Central Park. There's an amazing nest of black-capped chickadees near the reservoir."

What Mickey wanted to say was, "No way! That sounds deadly boring!" but instead she replied, "Awesome."

"You'll sleep in here," Olive said, pointing to a small room off the kitchen. It was painted banana yellow.

"It's really pretty," Mickey said, pretending to like it. She wheeled in Edith and set her tackle box filled with threads, needles, pins, zippers, and scissors on the small nightstand. No matter where she went, she found something to add to it: a cool stud or grommet, an interesting snap or vintage button. It was her magic box for designing.

"It used to be my office, but I suppose I can make do," Olive said with a sigh. "I didn't think you'd be bringing so much *stuff* with you." She helped Mickey carry in a huge tote bag that weighed a ton. "What's in here?"

"My steamer, my iron, my muslin for draping patterns…"

"I see," Olive said. "Your mother didn't mention that you'd come with all of this."

"Thank you so much for letting me stay with you," Mickey said, plopping down on the edge of the bed. Like the walls, the cover, sheets, and pillowcases were all yellow as well—with more birds on them.

"I'm really good at sewing and dyeing fabric," Mickey mentioned. "Maybe I could do some pretty new curtains and a quilt…"

Olive frowned. "You'll do nothing of the sort!"

Mickey gulped. She had been there only five minutes and already managed to irritate her aunt.

"The room is great—really," she tried to explain. "It's just not exactly my style."

Olive eyed Mickey's black leather jacket, gray tank top, jean shorts, and purple Dr. Martens.

"Yes, well, I could see that it might not be. But I just went to Macy's and purchased that bedding."

Now Mickey felt guilty. "Oh, I love it. Really. You have great taste."

That seemed to calm her aunt down.

"I'm really hungry from the train ride." Mickey tried to

change the subject. "Can we maybe go out and get some pizza or something?"

"I'm a vegan," Olive sniffed. "And I don't allow any processed food in my home."

Mickey took that to mean no to a slice. "Okay, then what would *you* like to eat?" She regretted the words as soon as they came out of her mouth.

"I have some leftover black bean soup and spinach chickpea curry," her aunt replied.

"Yum," Mickey gulped. "Sounds delish."

"Then wash up," Olive ordered her. She presented Mickey with a hand towel from the linen closet and a small bottle of hand sanitizer. "I suggest you carry this with you at all times in your backpack. Schools are full of germs, and I don't want you bringing them home…"

She wandered off to start heating up their dinner.

Mickey took out her phone and began texting her mom: Help! Aunt Olive is making vegetarian slop for dinner, and she's a germophobic bird-watcher! But before she hit *send*, she reconsidered. The last thing she wanted her mom to do was worry—or worse, say, "I told ya so."

Everything GR8 with Aunt Olive! she typed and sent.

Even if it wasn't, she had to remind herself that she

was here in NYC at last, following her dreams. And if that meant she had to eat beans and tofu for the next two hundred or so days of school, then she would do it and never complain. Some dreams were worth making sacrifices for.

First-Day Jitters

After spending the weekend with her aunt, Mickey concluded that Olive wasn't *that* bad—at least not as bad as her mom made her out to be. She was just a bit uptight. It was hard for Mickey to understand how she and her mom could be sisters, much less fraternal twins. They had the same curly, strawberry-blond hair, though her mom highlighted hers and wore it long and loose and Olive pinned hers back in a tight bun. She recognized her aunt's eyes as well—they were emerald green, just like her mom's. Too bad she hid them behind thick tortoiseshell glasses. Then there was her style: Olive looked like she had stepped out of a time warp. She wore a ruffled pink blouse, long pearls, and an A-line brown skirt. Maybe she was going for a retro fifties vibe? It was the opposite of her mom's ripped jeans and vintage rock T-shirts. Maybe there had been some mistake and they were switched at birth? Maybe her granny Gertrude got confused and accidentally picked up the wrong baby in the park one day?

Olive was also a neat freak who insisted that everything be "spic and span" and in its place.

"Mackenzie, clean up after yourself!" she scolded when Mickey left her sketchbook and colored pencils on the kitchen table. No one called her Mackenzie; her mom only used it when she was mad at her. It was a name she barely recognized or answered to. But as many times as she corrected Aunt Olive, she insisted on calling her by her "proper name."

"Mom calls me Mickey, and I call her Jordana sometimes," she tried to explain.

"I don't care what you call your mom or she calls you. And you call me Aunt Olive out of respect," she warned her.

Mickey wrinkled her nose. "Really? Mom says she called you Olliegator when you were little. I think that's cute."

Olive pursed her lips. "I'm an adult," she replied sternly. Aunt Olive was an executive assistant at a big law firm, and she took everything very seriously. "Your mother needs to grow up."

But that was exactly what Mickey loved about her mom—how she was such a free spirit and never cared what anyone thought or said about her. Mickey tried her hardest to be that way, but sometimes it was hard.

For the first day of FAB, she set her alarm for six o'clock so she would have time to style her outfit properly. She was proud of how it had all come together. She'd taken a beaten-up denim jacket from a thrift shop and dyed it black before adding crocheted doilies for trim at the collars and cuffs. It said exactly what she wanted it to say about her: "I'm edgy but feminine." And wasn't that what fashion was all about? Not just a trend or a style, but a reflection of who you are and how you're feeling? That was what Mickey loved about designing the most, and what she had written on her FAB application:

I love how you can speak volumes with a single stitch. Fashion should be fearless! I want to be a designer who always colors outside the lines and thinks outside of the box...

She was pretty sure Aunt Olive didn't see it that way. Her idea of taking a fashion risk was wearing a skirt that was hemmed above the knee.

"Does it really go together?" she asked, noticing how Mickey had paired her jacket with a white tank top and bike shorts, both of which were splatter-painted with green-and-yellow drips.

"It isn't supposed to *go*," Mickey told her. "It's supposed to look creative, which is what FAB is all about. Pushing the envelope!"

She added a pair of green cat-eye sunglasses.

"Well, it's colorful." Her aunt sighed. "I'll give you that. And so is your hair. Good heavens!"

Mickey had created green stripes in her long, wavy, blond hair with hair chalk.

"Now for the finishing touch!" she said. "No outfit is complete without accessories!" She slipped her feet into a pair of black high-top sneakers, tied the yellow laces, and grabbed her bag.

"What is that?" her aunt asked, scratching her head. She squinted to make out the words on Mickey's tote.

"It used to say 'Louis Vuitton'—it's a bag you keep a really fancy expensive bag in. Which if you ask me, is pretty silly," Mickey explained.

Olive seemed puzzled. "You mean a dust bag? You made that out of a dust bag?"

Mickey spun the tote around. "Two of them, actually!" The other side read "PRADA."

"What? How? Why?" Olive asked.

"Well, it's perfectly good flannel," Mickey replied. "And

don't you think it's kinda funny? A statement about recycling? I used two leather belts for the straps and jazzed it up with some studding at the seams. It cost me about four dollars total at the flea market!"

She threw the bag over her shoulder and glanced at the clock. It was eight, and the school bus would be along shortly to pick her up on the corner.

"Your breakfast is ready," Olive said, handing her a glass of green sludge. This was worse then yesterday's quinoa and fruit concoction! She missed her mom's breakfasts of leftover Chinese takeout omelets or cold pizza. But Aunt Olive insisted she start the first day of school with "something healthy and nutritious."

"Do you have any chocolate milk?" she asked, getting up to check the fridge for something edible.

"This is better for you. It's fresh kale, celery, cucumber, ginger, and a touch of agave. It's delicious." She took a big sip of her own glass and licked her lips.

Mickey wrinkled her nose. It didn't look or smell delicious. "I think I'll grab something in the cafeteria," she said, pushing the glass away. "I'm too nervous to eat."

It wasn't *entirely* a lie. She was pretty terrified for her first day at FAB. Just then, Mickey's phone rang.

"All ready to conquer the world?" her mom asked.

"I think so, Jordana," she replied.

"Ah, I see. We're trying to sound very mature this morning. Send me a picture of the first-day outfit and call me tonight. I want to hear all the deets."

Mickey smiled. Her mom was trying to sound cool. "I will. Love you."

As the bus pulled up to the corner of Columbus Avenue, Mickey took a deep breath. This wasn't just the first day of FAB. It was the first day of the rest of her life. The first day of everything.

Sew FAB

The trip over the Brooklyn Bridge had taken longer than she expected, but Mickey didn't mind the bumper-to-bumper traffic or the honking horns. She was taking it all in: the sights and sounds that were New York City, fashion capital of the world! As the kids filed off the school bus, she was able to get a better look at what they were all wearing. She saw several Abercrombie hoodies, a few Brandy Melville graphic tees, countless pairs of Superga sneakers in boring tennis white.

What happened to pushing the envelope? she wondered. *Where was the creativity? The originality? They all looked like carbon copies of each other.*

"Nice hair," a girl snickered as she pushed past her with her posse. She was dressed in a simple jean skirt and pink graphic T-shirt that read "#pretty."

"Didn't you get the memo? It's not Halloween!"

Mickey walked up the steps to the school's huge gray concrete and glass doors. Even the building looked boring.

A voice behind her read her mind. "You were expecting something a bit more artsy, right?" She turned to see a short boy carrying a purple tote bag that was almost as big as he was. She noticed the bag had holes in the sides.

"I guess," Mickey replied. "I'm not sure what I was expecting."

"You're new," he said, climbing the steps. "Sixth-grader?"

Mickey nodded. "You?"

"Seventh. I'm Javen Cumberland." He dug in the pocket of his jeans and pulled out a business card. Mickey read it: "JC Canine Couture."

"You design for dogs?" She gasped.

The boy raised an eyebrow. "I wouldn't be so judgy, Miss 'I colored my hair to look like a salad…'"

"It's green, okay? I like green."

He chuckled. "Apparently. But your bag rocks. Really."

Mickey smiled and noticed that his bag was moving. "Is there something in there?" she whispered.

He unzipped the top of his tote, and a tiny, wet nose poked out. "Madonna the Chihuahua, meet…what's your name again?"

"Mickey. Mickey Williams."

"Don't tell anyone, okay?" he said, zipping Madonna back into her home. "No dogs on FAB property. Mr. Kaye would have a fit. But she's kind of my mascot. She goes where I go."

"I promise. Your secret is safe with me," Mickey replied. "But who's Mr. Kaye?"

"Only the toughest Apparel Arts teacher in the entire school."

"Oh." Mickey gulped.

"You definitely want to watch out for him…and those two." He motioned to the curb, where a large, white stretch limo was pulling up. A girl and a boy stepped out, waving to the crowd of students as if they were royalty.

Mickey wrinkled her nose. "Who are they?"

"The Lee twins. They're in my grade. Their mom is Bridget Lee, wedding designer to the stars."

Mickey whistled through her teeth. "Whoa! She's super-famous. She did Jessica Simpson's wedding gown!"

"Exacterooni," Javen replied. "So steer clear of Jade and Jake. Or as I prefer to call them, Tweedle Mean and Tweedle Meaner."

Mickey stared at the pair. They looked fairly normal, if not a bit fancy for the first day of school. Jade was wearing white lace shorts and a white chiffon halter top. Her long black hair was pulled back in a rhinestone headband that looked like a tiara. Jake was dressed in a white linen suit with a baby-blue polo shirt underneath.

When Jade was done air-kissing all her friends on both cheeks, she took her pink crushed-velvet Chanel backpack from the limo driver and slung it over one shoulder.

"Wow. That bag's not even available yet. It's in the fall/spring collection," Mickey remarked.

"You know your runway—that's a plus," the boy told her before rushing off to his first class. "Good luck on your first day, Green Girl."

Mickey tried to decipher her schedule and find her way around FAB's long and winding hallways. There were six floors with design studios on each. In the basement was the FAB auditorium, complete with a real runway worthy of New York or Paris Fashion Week.

Besides the basic middle school classes—math, science, English, and language—there were two design classes every day. Her Apparel Arts class was on the very top floor.

She reached the sixth-floor landing, panting from the climb up all those stairs, and took her seat in studio 6A. She heaved a sigh of relief: she'd made it on time.

"Take out your textbooks," the teacher instructed the class. "We'll begin with naming the five oceans." She unrolled a large world map and pointed to it.

"Um, excuse me," Mickey interrupted her. "Is this Apparel Arts 1?"

"This is world geography," the woman replied. "Try the room at the end of the hall."

Mickey gathered her books and raced to studio 6B. Class was already in session, so she knocked gently on the door before opening it. "Excuse me"—she peered in—"is *this* Apparel Arts 1?"

A dapper gentleman with graying hair, a mustache, and a plaid bow tie peered at her over the tops of his wire-rimmed spectacles. "And you might be?"

"Lost. I'm lost. I went to another room and they told me I was in the wrong place."

The man tapped his mechanical pencil against his chin. "You don't say? Well then, congratulations. You've come to the right place. Take a seat."

He pointed to a drafting table a few feet from his desk

with a dress form set up next to it. Mickey looked around the room and noticed the rest of the class was whispering and giggling.

"Is there a problem?" the teacher asked.

"No, no problem," Mickey said, sliding into her seat. She could feel the eyes on the back of her neck.

"Good. Then we can begin. I am Mr. Kaye, and this is Apparel Arts 1. Everyone in this class is either new to FAB—or flunked my class last semester." He stared in disapproval at the boy sitting in the desk next to Mickey. "Gabriel can attest to that."

The boy sunk in his seat. Mickey realized this was the teacher JC had warned her about, and he wasn't kidding!

"Over the course of the semester, we shall be learning the elements of design. Does anyone want to tell me what they are?"

Mickey shyly raised her hand. "Yes, the late girl," Mr. Kaye replied. "Go on."

"I'd say color, silhouette, texture, and line," she answered.

"And I'd say you are correct," Mr. Kaye responded. "And by line, what do we mean?"

Gabriel's hand went up. "Well, there can be seam lines and pattern lines—like the way stripes line up."

"Line is the most complex element," Mr. Kaye explained. "It can create shape and illusion. It can be structural or decorative. It can create a mood and a message."

Mickey tried her best to write down every word her teacher said—it was all so fascinating!

"Besides learning the elements of design, you will sketch and create three looks based on themes I assign you," Mr. Kaye continued. "I will grade them on a scale from one to four, four being the highest. Then, at the end of the semester, we will total up the points, and three students— one each from grades six, seven, and eight—will present a four-piece capsule collection on the runway before a panel of judges."

He stood up in front of the SMART Board and drew a big number 1 on it. "Challenge number one will be due in class tomorrow."

"Tomorrow?" Gabriel groaned. "That soon?"

"There is no wasting time in my class," Mr. Kaye insisted. "I want to see how talented and creative you all are. Or not." He looked around the room at the terrified faces.

"You!" He pointed to a girl dressed all in black leather in the back row. He looked at his class list, hunting for her name. "South East?"

Gabriel chuckled. "Is that a name or an address?"

"Cool it!" a boy behind him whispered. "Don't you know who she is? That's Laser East's daughter."

"The rapper?" Gabriel replied.

The boy nodded. "The one who's married to the reality TV star."

Mr. Kaye was busy quizzing South on what she thought about the World Hunger Council.

"To design you must first understand your client and what he or she wants and needs," he explained. "South, what do you suppose the World Hunger Council would be looking for in a T-shirt?"

The girl shifted nervously in her seat. "I dunno," she said quietly. "Something that makes people donate money I guess?"

Mr. Kaye nodded. "Yes, they would want a message that inspires people to give to their organization. What else?"

He strolled to the front of the room and looked straight at Mickey. "Mackenzie Williams," he read off his list.

"It's actually Mickey."

Mr. Kaye furrowed his brow. "Pardon?"

"It's Mickey. No one calls me Mackenzie except my aunt Olive."

Mr. Kaye cleared his throat. "*Mickey*," he continued. "What do you think the client would be looking for in a garment?"

Mickey took a deep breath and tried to think of something—anything—smart to say. "Food. They'd be looking for food."

The class erupted in laughter, and Mr. Kaye took off his glasses and rubbed his temples.

"Silence!" he commanded. "Miss Williams has a valid point. The World Hunger Council is definitely looking for food. But that is stating the obvious."

A girl seated in the front row raised her hand, and Mickey noticed a stack of silver bangles on her wrist. She wasn't sure, but they looked like they were made out of the tops of soda cans.

"Jewelry designer?" she whispered to Gabriel.

"For sure. Check out the humungo hoop earrings."

Mr. Kaye squinted at the girl's name on the class list. "Marzipan?" he asked.

Again, the class roared with laughter.

"It's *Mar-sa-leen*," she replied, unfazed. "But Mars is fine—as in the planet."

"And your last name?" Mr. Kaye said, making a note on his roster.

"Just Mars. I'm trying to create my own jewelry line out of recycled materials, and I thought 'Jewels from Mars' sounded a lot better than 'Stuff by Marceline Lipnicki.'"

"Indeed," Mr. Kaye commented. "Mars it is."

Gabriel had to practically cover his mouth with his hands to stop from cracking up. "We have an alien from outer space in our class!" he said, snickering.

Mr. Kaye shot him a mean look. "If everyone is quite finished speaking out of turn, Mars had something to add to the discussion."

"I wanted to know if we could accessorize the shirt for our assignment?" she asked.

"You can—for extra credit. Although you must stay within the budget."

He wrote the number ten on the SMART Board and drew a circle around it. "Ten dollars. No more. Extra credit if you use less."

"That's impossible," South protested. "I was going to do leather embellishments."

"Then you'll just have to get creative," their teacher insisted. "Creativity counts."

He handed each student a plain white T-shirt. "Feel free to rummage through the scrap box and look around your home for materials that you have already at your disposal." He pointed to a huge plastic bin next to his desk brimming with fabric swatches and bits of trim. "I'll give you the rest of the period to sketch."

Mickey started to get up and join the rest of the class pulling scraps from the box. Then she stopped herself. That was too easy. Her design had to be unique, innovative, something Mr. Kaye had never seen before. But what?

"This is a nightmare." Gabriel groaned, looking at the pile of scraps he'd managed to wrestle out of Mars's hands. "That E.T. girl practically broke my arm for the blue silk-cashmere blend!"

"Did you get it?" Mickey asked.

He waved a small torn patch of fabric in the air. "Well, I got a piece of it."

While everyone else was busy sketching, Mickey sat staring at the blank sheet of paper and chewing her pencil eraser.

"Designer's block already?" her teacher asked, making a *tsk-tsk* sound as he peered over Mickey's shoulder.

"I guess I'm just stuck trying to come up with something original," she replied. "What should I do?"

"What you came to FAB to do," Mr. Kaye said with a dismissive wave of his hand. "Be a fashion designer."

Food for Thought

On the bus ride home, Mickey thought hard about her Apparel Arts homework assignment, closing her eyes and trying to picture what her shirt might look like. She saw swirls of color and an array of textures—but what were they? She was completely lost in thought until a banana peel came sailing through the air and landed on her head.

The boys in the last row of the bus were having a food fight.

"Settle down!" the bus driver barked. "No throwing garbage on my bus!"

Mickey was about to stand up and hurl the peel back at the unruly group, when a brilliant idea suddenly came to her. She just needed to get home before Aunt Olive!

When the bus finally pulled up to her corner, Mickey jumped off and bounded up the stairs to her aunt's apartment. She let herself in and headed straight for the kitchen. She glanced at the bird clock on the wall—it was four fifteen. Her aunt would be home from work by five thirty, so there was no time to waste or even sketch. She pulled the white T-shirt out of her backpack and threw it down on the kitchen table. Then she began rummaging through the fridge and cupboard shelves. Amazingly, she found just what she needed: beets, raspberries, blueberries, and a bag of dried cranberries. She crumpled the shirt into a large mixing bowl, then began crushing the beets and berries till the garment was streaked with purple, red, and blue smudges. Using a needle to pierce the cranberries, she secured them with thread to the neckline of the shirt.

She stood back and admired her handiwork. It still needed something. But what? She opened the fridge again and spied the perfect thing: a huge head of red cabbage. She quickly stripped off the leaves and sewed them to the hem of the shirt. From a distance, they looked like purple-and-white ruffles.

Just then, she heard Olive's key in the door. She quickly swept all the leftover food and mashed berries into the garbage and tried to wipe the red stains off the countertop.

"Mackenzie? Are you home?" her aunt called.

"Um, I'm in the kitchen. Be out in a sec!" She carefully folded the shirt into a plastic bag and stuffed it in her backpack just as her aunt was walking into the kitchen.

"You can help me sauté the red cabbage for dinner," Olive said, going to the sink to wash up.

Mickey gulped. "The red cabbage?"

Olive opened the fridge and searched. "Yes, I was sure I put it right here in the crisper."

Mickey thought quickly. "Oh, *that* red cabbage. I'm so sorry, Aunt Olive. I ate it for my after-school snack."

Olive stared. "You ate an entire head of red cabbage? Raw?"

"Yeah, it was really yummy. I couldn't help myself."

"Well," Olive replied, wiping her hands on her apron. "I'll just have to run out to the grocery and get another. And if you like it so much, I'll get you one for tomorrow as well."

Mickey breathed a huge sigh of relief. She waited till she heard the door slam to call her mom at Wanamaker's and fill her in on her first day.

"How was it, Mickey Mouse?" Her mom was dying to know.

"It was good, just different," Mickey explained. "I'm really excited for my Apparel Arts assignment that's due tomorrow. I think I rocked it."

"Of course you did," her mom replied. "I would expect nothing less. Did you make friends?"

"Um, yeah, a couple. This boy JC seemed nice."

"Is Aunt Olive driving you up the walls yet?" her mom pushed. "Is she making you eat kale milk shakes for breakfast?"

"She just went out to get us some dinner," Mickey said. "Don't worry, Jordana. I'm fine."

She heard a client in the background asking her mom something about waterproof mascara. "Gotta run, Mouse! Call ya later!"

Convincing her mom FAB was fab was one thing; convincing her best friend was another.

"Are the kids stuck up?" Annabelle wanted to know when Mickey called her next. "I bet they are, right?"

Mickey told her all about Jade and Jake's grand entrance, and how JC carried his Chihuahua everywhere. "There are kids named Mars and South East in my design class," she added.

"They sound really weird," Annabelle said. "I got my

schedule today, and it's awesome. I have Dance for first Arts Rotation!"

"Cool," Mickey said, trying to sound excited for her friend. If she had stayed in Philly, they would have been walking to school together every day.

"Oh! And my mom took Becky Adams and me for froyo after school! They've got this awesome new flavor that tastes exactly like chocolate milk!"

Mickey missed Annabelle. And froyo. And chocolate milk. "So you and Becky are now besties?" she asked, fingering the silver thimble charm around her neck. "I thought you hated her because she made fun of your braces last year?"

"Nah, she's okay. We share a locker, and she's in my Spanish and math classes."

Mickey nodded. "Sounds cool."

"Well, I gotta run, Mick. I have tons of homework!" She hung up before Mickey could say good-bye.

Olive walked back into the apartment and placed two red cabbages on the kitchen table. "I had to hike all the way to

90th Street to get organic ones," she said, out of breath from climbing the stairs. Then she noticed Mickey's long face.

"What's wrong?"

"Nothing. My best friend just seems really busy."

Olive handed her a pot to put the cabbage in. "You know what they say, 'Out of sight, out of mind...'" her aunt reminded her. "People have to get on with their lives whether or not you're there."

Mickey knew that was true. She didn't expect her mom to stop working or Annabelle to stop going to their favorite froyo place. But she also didn't expect to miss them so much.

"How was your first day of school?" Olive asked. "Everything you thought it would be?"

Mickey didn't feel like fibbing anymore. "It was hard. I couldn't find my classes, and the kids thought I was weird and kind of ignored me." She waited for her aunt to say something, anything, to make her feel better.

Olive pursed her lips. "I'm not sure I'm the best person to give you advice, Mackenzie. I've never been a mother, and I don't have very many friends."

Well, that was true...

"But I do know that most birds will eventually find a flock to fly with. Give it time."

A Nose for Style

The next day, Mickey couldn't wait till third period to present her World Hunger shirt. She made sure she dressed the part: a pale-blue vintage silk blouse over red plaid leggings and mismatched sneakers—one blue, one red. She topped it off with a blue feathered fascinator hat—just like she'd seen Kate Middleton wear on many a royal occasion. The outfit made her feel regal and smart at the same time. Yet when she climbed on the bus, the whispers started.

"What is she wearing on her head?" one boy asked, snickering. "It looks like a dead pigeon."

"And who wears two different colored sneakers?" another girl remarked. "That is so elementary school!"

Mickey pretended not to hear, but the comments hurt. When she got to her Apparel Arts class, things weren't any better.

"Do you own a mirror?" Mars asked her. "I mean seriously—what are you wearing?"

Mickey knew what she wanted to say: "I don't care what you think about my style, because that's just it—it's *my* style!" Instead, she shrugged. "I was trying something a little different."

"A little different?" South chuckled. "That's putting it mildly! Ouch! It hurts my eyes just to look at you!"

Thankfully, Mr. Kaye walked in before anyone else could poke fun at her outfit. "Take out your homework assignments," he instructed them.

Mickey opened her backpack and dug inside for her shirt. She noticed that something smelled sour as she pulled it out, but she decided to put it on and model it anyway.

"What *is* that?" Mars asked, checking out her work. "Is it tie-dye?"

"Kinda," Mickey replied. "But all natural—I used fruit."

Gabriel pushed in to get a closer look, then suddenly backed away. "It's not bad looking, but what's that smell?"

South sniffed Mickey. "OMG! I thought I stepped in something, but it's your project!"

Mickey noticed that her cabbage trim had wilted and

did smell a bit like spoiled coleslaw. In fact, her whole backpack did and now so did she.

Mr. Kaye clapped his hands together. "All right, who's ready to present first?" he asked, rubbing his palms together. "I'm eager to see what you've come up with." Mickey noticed that everyone had put their shirts on the dress forms next to their desks. No one else was modeling their look but her.

Gabriel sat back down at his desk and fanned the air with his folder. "I'll go first," he volunteered. "If I can be excused after. The smell of her homework is making me wanna barf!"

Mr. Kaye wrinkled his nose. "Something does smell a bit foul in here," he commented, sniffing around Mickey's desk. "Good heavens! What is that odor?"

Mickey felt like she was back in fourth grade all over again being forced to defend her spring skirt in home ec class. No, her T-shirt didn't look like everyone else's. And yes, it was a bit wilted. But it was one hundred percent original—didn't that count for something?

Mr. Kaye covered his nose with a handkerchief but continued to inspect Mickey's design. He motioned for her to rotate. "This dyeing technique—what is it?"

"Berry juice. I crushed berries into the fabric. And those are dried cranberries for the piping around the neck and cabbage leaves for the ruffle trim. I wanted my shirt to be completely made from food to show how important it is to the world."

"That is so gross!" South exclaimed. "Who uses spoiled food on a shirt?"

"It wasn't spoiled when I sewed it on yesterday," Mickey insisted. "I guess I didn't think about what would happen if I kept it in my bag overnight."

Mr. Kaye borrowed Gabriel's folder to fan the air. "Let's move on, shall we? And Miss Williams, please take off your design and deposit it in the trash outside of the room." He cracked open the window and inhaled some fresh air. Sadly, Mickey took the shirt off and placed it in the garbage can. When she returned to her seat, her cheeks were red with embarrassment.

No one had used food instead of fabric. Mars manipulated patches of different colored fabric to make a world map and accessorized with a matching macramé necklace; Gabriel drew a globe on his tee with fabric markers and used the blue scraps he wrestled away from Mars to create letters that spelled out "FEED ME" on the back. South sewed a hundred-dollar bill smack in the middle of her shirt.

"It's a bit minimalist, don't you think?" Mr. Kaye asked her. "What does it say to you?"

South stepped back and admired her work. "It says *money*. Which is what the World Hunger Council really wants, isn't it?"

Mr. Kaye thought it over. "I suppose so. But next time, I'd like to see you make more of an effort in your assignment. And I'm deducting points for going over the ten-dollar budget."

South frowned. "But the hundred-dollar bill didn't cost me anything! My dad just gave it to me."

As the students packed up to get to their next class, Mr. Kaye called Mickey over to his desk.

"I know you're disappointed with the outcome of your first assignment," he told her. "But part of being a successful designer is considering how the market will react," he said. "Clearly, your design was not well received."

Mickey didn't know what to say. It had seemed like such an amazing idea at the time to use food and not fabric to decorate her shirt.

"That said," Mr. Kaye continued, "I do wish to

commend you for your creativity. Your work shows great promise."

Mickey's eyes lit up. Was he telling her he liked it? Or even better, that she'd earned a four on this first assignment?

"I am giving you a three, but I know you'll do better next time. I see great potential in you, Miss Williams."

Even if she had earned some kind words from Mr. Kaye, Mickey couldn't help but notice the stares from her peers as she walked into the crowded sixth- and seventh-grade lunch period.

In the center of the room, she spied Jade and Jake surrounded by a posse of kids. South had already elbowed into the group. Mickey assumed it had something to do with her bragging about her dad's new duet with Jay-Z—or maybe she gave Jade the hundred-dollar bill from her T-shirt?

When Mickey walked by with her lunch tray, the group grew silent.

"That's her," she heard South telling Jade. "Don't let her sit here. She stinks like rotten cabbage!"

But instead, Jade called after her. "Do you want to sit with us?" she asked Mickey, shoving her brother over to make room.

"Um, sure, I guess," Mickey hesitated.

As she edged closer, Jade suddenly slammed her binder down on the empty seat. "Oops, sorry! No fashion faux pas allowed!" The kids at the table all roared with laughter.

Mickey didn't know what to do—hiding in the first-floor girls' bathroom with her lunch tray seemed like a definite possibility. Then she noticed JC waving at her from a corner table.

"I can squeeze you in," he teased as Mickey took a seat at the otherwise empty table.

He noticed she wasn't smiling. "Bad time in Apparel Arts?" he pressed her for details.

"Epic fail. I don't wanna talk about it."

"You don't have to," he replied. "Gabriel filled me in." He sniffed the air. "But he wasn't kidding—you really do kinda stink."

Mickey shot him a look. "You're not making me feel any better."

"I'm not the one who told you to take a bath in eau de cabbage," he joked.

"I didn't do it on purpose," Mickey said. "I was just trying to stand out from the crowd."

JC patted her feathery blue hat. "Well, mission accomplished. You stick out, all right. Look around, Mickey. Do you see anyone who looks like you?"

Mickey surveyed the room—there wasn't a silly hat in sight and not a single pair of mismatched shoes. Maybe she had gone a *tad* overboard with her outfit and her homework assignment.

"I'm not saying it's a bad thing to be a fashion original," JC continued. "Not if you're Lady Gaga, for example. Or the world's coolest Chihuahua…" He tossed part of his meatloaf sandwich into his bag to feed Madonna. "I'm just saying sometimes less is more. Dial it down a notch."

"I don't know how to dial it down," Mickey admitted.

"When's your next assignment for Mr. Kaye due?"

Mickey checked her class schedule. "Three weeks."

"Great!" JC said, dipping a french fry in a puddle of ketchup on his plate. "That gives us tons of time."

"For what?" Mickey asked.

"For an extreme makeover!"

8

Mickey 2.0

When JC offered to help Mickey, she had no idea what she was getting herself into. He invited her over to his apartment the next day after school.

"Okay, first things first," he said, ushering her into his room-turned-design studio. "We need to rethink your branding."

He opened his bag, and Madonna leaped out. She took a seat in her pink leopard-print dog bed and settled in for a snooze.

"You made all of these?" Mickey asked, looking through Madonna's basket filled with doggy couture.

"Do you like them?" JC asked. "This one's my favorite." He held up a black satin dog coat covered in white embroidered skulls. "Very Alexander McQueen, don't you think?"

Mickey nodded. "Very. And this pink quilted vest is so Chanel."

"I know. I'm a doggy design genius."

Mickey giggled. JC certainly had a ton of confidence. She used to feel that way about her designs too. But during her first week at FAB, nothing seemed to be going right. She was dressed in all blue today, right down to the navy streaks in her hair and her nail polish. It reflected her mood.

"So let's talk about who you are," JC said, pulling out a sketchbook and a pencil.

"Do you have amnesia? I'm Mickey Williams," she answered.

"No, I mean, who do you want the world to see you as? I, for example, do not want to be regarded as Javen Linus Cumberland. Who would buy anything with that label? So I rebranded myself as JC Canine Couture. Get it?"

"Linus?" Mickey chuckled. "I can see why you changed your name."

"So who are you?" he pushed her. "As a designer?"

Mickey looked puzzled. "I'm not sure. I'm just me."

"Okay, then let's deal with appearances first," he said, handing her a towel. "No more Cruella De Vil hair. Wash out those streaks."

"Really? Is this necessary?" she complained.

JC held up a hand. "Do you want people to think of you as more than the Cabbage Patch Kid?"

"Fine," Mickey said, grabbing the towel out of his hand and walking to the bathroom. "I'll try anything." She scrubbed her hair in the sink and blew it dry so it fell in soft waves around her shoulders. When she came back, JC nodded in approval.

"Blond is definitely your color," he said. "No more trying to hide it with hair chalk."

He handed her a garment bag. "Try this on for size. I usually sew for pups, not people, but I think I did a decent job."

Mickey unzipped the bag. Inside was a teal one-shouldered dress. The fabric was soft and shimmery and draped to perfection.

"Wow. It's really beautiful. You made this?" she asked.

"I saw something similar on the Paris Runway reports—Beyoncé bought it."

Mickey admired the delicate stitches and attention to detail. "It's amazing, JC, but I just don't think it's me."

JC took the dress off the hanger and handed it to her. "It is you. The *new* you. Try it on."

She ducked into the bathroom and slipped the dress over her head. It fit her like a glove. When she looked in the mirror, she barely recognized the person staring back at her.

JC knocked on the door. "How does it look?"

Mickey opened the door and stepped out. JC's jaw dropped.

"Wow. You look like a supermodel. This oughta give Jade and her cloniacs something to talk about tomorrow!"

"Oh no. I can't go to school like this!" Mickey exclaimed.

"Oh, yes you can!" JC insisted. "And we'll need a really good story to go with it." He flopped down on his beanbag chair to think of a plan. "I know! Your real name is Kenzie Wills, and your father is a famous fashion designer. You were just trying to hide your true identity from the paparazzi!"

Mickey sighed. "My father is a bass player who I haven't seen in ten years."

JC shrugged. "So? A little white lie never hurt anyone. Right, Madonna?"

The tiny dog yawned in approval.

"How would my dad be a designer that no one has ever heard of?" Mickey asked.

"He designs very far away—in Finland. That's it! He's a Finnish fashion star! To the royal family of Finland!"

Mickey shook her head. "And you think Jade is going to buy that? Or South or any of them?"

JC grinned. "With a little gossip, they'll buy anything. And I know just how to spread the word."

He went to his laptop and typed in a website address: www.sewfab.com.

"What is that?" Mickey asked.

"A little style blog that everyone at FAB worships. No one knows who writes it—it's a Gossip Girl kinda thing. Very secretive. But you can send in your tips. Which is exactly what I'm going to do…"

Mickey watched nervously as JC's fingers flew across the keyboard. When he was finished, he showed her what he'd written:

What new student is really the daughter of Finnish fashion royalty in disguise hiding out from the press? Watch for a grand entrance at FAB tomorrow morning!

9

★ Introducing Kenzie Wills! ★

JC had insisted that Mickey not take the bus Friday morning to school. He insisted she needed "a big reveal."

Think, "I'm Kenzie Wills, design diva!" he texted her bright and early. And don't forget to ditch the high-tops and wear my mom's heels that I gave you! C U soon!

Mickey knew she had to play the part of Kenzie Wills or no one would believe her. So she tried it out on Aunt Olive first.

"Morning, Auntie," Mickey said, gliding into the kitchen in her new dress.

"You look...*different*," Olive noted. "No turquoise streaks in your hair today to match your dress?"

Mickey wrinkled her nose. "That is *so* yesterday."

Olive shrugged. "I thought yesterday was blue streaks. I can't keep up with you, Mackenzie."

"Few can," Mickey said, pouring herself a glass of grape-fruit juice. "It isn't easy to be a fashion icon, you know."

"I wouldn't want to try!" Olive replied. "For what it's worth, I like your dress. It's more conservative than the other outfits you've been wearing."

"I dialed it down a notch," Mickey said, checking her look one last time in the mirror before she headed out to the corner to wait for JC. "*Hay hay!*"

Olive looked puzzled. "*Hay hay?* What does that mean?"

"It's *good-bye* in Finnish," Mickey explained. JC had also suggested she look up a few Finnish phrases on Google Translate. Just in case.

"Oh. *Hay hay,*" Olive replied. "Have a good day."

As she stood outside waiting for her friend, Mickey tried her best not to fidget or pace. Besides, walking in these high heels made her feet kill! If she was going to pull this off, she needed to be cool and confident—not to mention fluent in Finnish!

A long, black limo pulled up and honked its horn. A chauffeur stepped out and held the door open for her.

"Um, I think there's been some mistake…" Mickey said. "This isn't my car."

A Chihuahua barked excitedly from the backseat.

"What are you waiting for, Mick? A royal invitation?" JC asked.

"How did you get this?" Mickey asked, climbing inside.

"My next-door neighbor drives for a car service in between acting gigs. He won't tell or charge us, right, Bogart?"

The chauffeur nodded. "It's good acting practice for me anyway—I've never played the role of a chauffeur to a celebrity before."

When they pulled up in front of FAB, Mickey's heart began to pound. JC ducked down so no one would see him in the limo with her.

"I don't know if I can do this," she told him.

"You can. Pretend it's a runway. Go out there and strut like a supermodel."

"These heels are too high. I'm gonna break my neck!" Mickey moaned. "And I feel naked without my moto jacket. Maybe I should go back home and change?"

"Out!" JC insisted. "You got this."

Mickey took a deep breath as Bogart opened the door to let her out.

"Good luck, Miss Wills," he said with a wink.

Mickey tried to smile. "Thanks. I'm gonna need it."

A crowd of students had already gathered around to

see who was arriving in a stretch limo. Sewfab.com had already blasted out the news, just as JC had said. Everyone was expecting a grand entrance of someone ultra chic and ultra famous.

Mickey saw Jade and South waiting at the curb. She expected them to snicker or throw something at her when she emerged. Instead, they stared.

As she slowly climbed the steps to the school's main entrance, she tried to make out the whispers.

"That must be her," said one girl. "I hear she lives in a castle in Finland."

"She's a gazillionaire," said another boy. "She's, like, richer than the Kardashians!"

Mickey couldn't believe they were talking about *her*. She was even more shocked when Jade ran up to her at her locker. "You," she addressed Mickey.

Mickey reminded herself to keep her cool and play her part.

"Me," she replied simply, grabbing her history textbook.

"Is it true?" Jade continued. "Are you some Finnish fashion princess or something?"

Mickey batted her eyelashes. "I have no idea what you're talking about. *Ahn-tehk-see.* Pardon me."

"Wait!" Jade called after her. "Was that Finnish? Are you speaking Finnish? So it's true? You're not really a fashion don't? You're a do in disguise?"

Mickey ignored her and walked away, even as Jade was shouting after her, "Hey, wanna sit at my table at lunch?"

JC was right. All it took was "rebranding" herself to make people like her. That and a little white lie or two...

When she took her seat in Apparel Arts, Gabriel pulled his chair closer to hers.

"What happened to you?" he whispered.

Mickey shrugged. "I'm sure I don't know what you're talking about."

"He means you don't look like a freak anymore," Mars volunteered.

"Aren't you afraid the paparazzi will stalk you if you're not incognito?" South asked.

"It doesn't bother you, does it?" Mickey asked her. "Your father is famous."

"But he's a rap singer, not the king of Finland!" Gabriel pointed out. "That's what I heard. Is it true? Are you Princess Mickey?"

Mickey had to giggle. It was amazing how quickly rumors spread and the facts became twisted, like a game of telephone with each person distorting the original message even more.

"It's Kenzie. Not Mickey," she said. "And I'm not supposed to talk about my personal life."

"Not even with your friends?" South continued. "You can trust us!"

"*Ahn-tehk-see*," Mickey said with a sigh. "I'm sorry. Rules are rules."

Even Mr. Kaye looked shocked when he walked in and spied Mickey's style transformation.

"Miss Williams?" he asked, putting his glasses on to get a better look. "I didn't recognize you."

Mickey hoped her teacher wasn't disappointed—he was the one who loved her creativity, and now she looked like just another Jade wannabe. "I just thought it was time for a change," she tried to explain. "Time to show everyone the real me, Kenzie Wills."

Mr. Kaye raised an eyebrow. "And you're sure this is the *real* you?"

Mickey nodded. "Uh-huh. I think so."

"Then you should appreciate your next fashion challenge assignment." He walked to the SMART Board and drew a 2 on it.

"Oh boy. Here it comes." Gabriel groaned.

"The theme is 'Everything Old Is New Again.' I would like you to take an item of clothing from another era and rework it so it feels fresh and modern."

"Where do we get the old outfit?" South asked.

"That's part of the challenge," their teacher explained. "Finding your inspiration."

For Mickey, the answer was simple: the flea market she and her mom loved to browse on Sunday mornings would have tons of vintage clothes.

"Your budget is twenty dollars. Good luck and good designing!"

At lunch, Jade practically threw her brother on the floor to make room next to her for Mickey.

"Sit here," she ushered her over. "It's the fashionista table."

Mickey slid in beside her and nibbled on her salad.

"So, what's Finnish Fashion Week like?" Jade asked her. "I go to Paris, Barcelona, and Milan every year with my mother, but I've never been to Finland."

"Oh, you know. Runways, supermodels, queens and

kings and stuff," Mickey said, pretending to yawn. "It's rather boring."

"Boring?" South gasped. "It sounds awesome. Can I go with you next time?"

Jade kicked her under the table.

"Ow!" South yelped. "You stabbed me with your stiletto!"

"If Kenzie is going to take anyone with her to Finnish Fashion Week, it's me," Jade said. "After all, fashion royalty should stick together, agreed?"

Mickey had to think fast. "Um, sorry. My dad has a very large staff and a very small private jet. No room for any extras on the flight to Helsinki."

"Oh! That's okay," Jade volunteered. "My mom has her own private jet too. I could just meet you there. Save me a seat in the front row?"

Mickey looked over at JC, who was sitting with Gabriel at another table. "Help me!" she mouthed.

"So, Kenzie," Jade said, putting an arm around her shoulder. "My mother is having a small get-together at her Madison Avenue boutique tomorrow night for a few VIP clients. I'd love for you to come. What do you say?"

Mickey couldn't believe it! She was invited to an

exclusive Bridget Lee party! But she'd promised her mom she'd come home to Philly for the weekend.

"I'd love to, but unfortunately, I have to hit the thrift shops and flea markets," Mickey said.

Jade's cheeks flushed red. "You what? Are you turning me down? To go shopping at Goodwill?"

"Sis, you've been dissed!" Jake chuckled. "Nice one, Kenzie!"

Mickey tried to backpedal. "No! I'm not dissing you, Jade. Really! I have this Apparel Arts assignment, and we're suppose to turn something old into something new and fab."

Jade's face softened. "Well, why didn't you say so? I know this amazing little resale shop down in the Village that has vintage Chanel, Gucci, Pucci. I'll take you there Saturday morning!"

Mickey tried to smile. How was she going to explain breaking her promise to her mom and Annabelle this weekend? And how was she ever going to keep up this masquerade?

10

Shop Till You Drop

"Hold on! Let me get this straight," JC shouted at Mickey over the phone. "Jadezilla is your new BFF?"

Mickey had called him immediately after school to give a recap of how her fellow FABers had reacted to her makeover.

"Well, she wants to take me shopping Saturday. I'm not sure what I'm going to tell my mom. She was counting on me to come home for the weekend."

"Just because Jade snaps her fingers doesn't mean you have to come running," he replied.

"I can't turn her down. She'll hate me all over again," Mickey reminded him.

JC sighed. "You're right. The show must go on. Call your mom and tell her you have a group project to work on and you can't get away. She'll understand."

"This is all your fault, you know," Mickey said. "It was

your idea to make me fit in at FAB. Now Jade wants me to take her to Finnish Fashion Week!"

JC chuckled. "What can I say? I'm just too good for my own good."

Once she convinced her mom that she needed to stay in the city—and swore she'd make it up to her next weekend—Mickey made plans to meet up with Jade and her mother's personal assistant Saturday morning. She was about to put on a pair of purple Dr. Martens and some paisley leggings with a black mesh sweater when she remembered what JC had told her: "Less is more." So instead, she chose a simple pair of jeans, a white tank, and a black pleather cropped jacket. She had to hunt in the back of her closet to actually find a pair of sneakers that matched, but finally located two black Converse.

"That's an interesting jacket," Jade said, feeling the sleeve as Mickey climbed into her limo. "Is it Prada?"

Mickey thought quickly. "No. It's a Finnish designer you've probably never heard of."

"Try me," Jade challenged her. "I know everything about couture. Right, Tinsley?"

The young assistant nodded enthusiastically. "Yes, of course, Miss Lee."

Mickey felt bad for the young woman. She couldn't think of a worse job than having to babysit Jade on a weekend.

"So what vintage store are we hitting?" Mickey tried to change the subject. "I'm sure you know all the best ones."

Jade grinned. "Of course I do. I thought we'd go to Retro Rags."

They piled out of the car, and Jade handed Tinsley her tote bag to carry.

"You still didn't tell me who designed your jacket," Jade reminded Mickey. "Friends shouldn't have any secrets."

"Um, his name is…" Mickey looked around the crowded downtown streets, trying to think of something, anything that Jade wouldn't instantly see through as a lie. Her eyes landed on a coffee and doughnut truck parked on the corner.

"Donutto. His name is Otto Donutto," she improvised.

"Oh, of course!" Jade fibbed. "I've heard of him. He's mega famous in fashion circles. I think my mom had dinner with him a few months ago."

Mickey breathed a sigh of relief. "Yeah, he's big."

"You think you could get him to send me some of his

pieces?" Jade asked, putting an arm around Mickey. "Pretty please? They're so unique."

Mickey chuckled to herself. She wasn't about to tell Jade that she'd gotten the jacket on sale at Wanamaker's for sixteen dollars. "I'll see what I can do."

When they walked into Retro Rags on West Broadway, Jade made a beeline for the racks of couture dresses.

"Do you see what I see?" she asked Mickey, pulling out a lavender cashmere halter-top dress.

Mickey knew it at first glance. "Halston from the seventies," she said. "It's amazing."

"It's mine!" Jade said, yanking it off the hanger and practically hurling it at Tinsley. "Put this on Mommy's charge."

Mickey caught a glimpse of the nine-hundred-and-fifty-dollar price tag and gasped.

"I know. It's a steal, don't ya think?" Jade asked. She piled another three dresses on the frazzled assistant: a Chanel pink knit, a navy Alaïa, and a black Versace safety-pin mini that the store clerk swore Lady Gaga had worn.

"Do you see anything you like for your Apparel Arts project?" Jade asked her.

There was *plenty* that Mickey liked in the store—hundreds of stunning looks that dated back as far as the

1920s. But there was nothing on those racks that she could afford.

"We can't go over twenty dollars for our budget." She remembered Mr. Kaye's warning. "So I don't think any of these will work."

Suddenly, she spied a collection of vintage rock T-shirts hanging over the counter. One looked familiar.

"Can I see that?" Mickey asked the store clerk, pointing to a black one with a gold compass design on it. It read "The Pioneers."

"That is so ugly," Jade sniffed. "Who ever heard of that band anyway?"

"I have," Mickey said, tracing the logo with her fingertips. "How much is it?"

"For you? Five bucks," the clerk replied. "No one's ever come in here asking for a Pioneers tour shirt."

Mickey smiled and handed him the money.

It may not have been a designer label with a thousand-dollar price tag, but to her it was priceless.

Blast from the Past

When it came to design challenge number two, Mickey wanted to make sure that this time her design didn't stink like sour cabbage again. So she called JC and asked him over to toss around some ideas. She laid out the rock tee on her kitchen table and studied it from every angle.

"So what are you going to do with it?" JC asked her. "I mean, it's a pretty boring shirt."

"It's not boring. It's very rare," Mickey defended her choice. "It's my dad's band."

"Oh," JC said softly. "Sorry. I didn't know."

"It's okay," Mickey said. She wasn't going to allow herself to get all sentimental over it. But she did think it had great potential for her project. She whipped out her sketchbook and began to draw. "I'm thinking of cutting the shirt down into a V-neck and replacing the cap sleeves with bat wings…"

JC watched as her pencil whipped across the page in a series of bold, black strokes. "What are you thinking for the bottom?"

"Definitely long. Maybe fringe? Maybe a train?"

"A train would be really dramatic and cutting edge," JC agreed with her. "What are you going to use for the fabric?"

Since she'd already spent five dollars on the shirt, that left a mere fifteen dollars for the maxi skirt and long sleeves—not to mention the studs she'd drawn in at the waist. "The compass and logo on the shirt is yellow. Maybe a yellow dupioni silk? Something with a bit of a sheen that would pop?"

"That fabric isn't cheap," JC pointed out. "I think you might have to reconsider."

Just then, Aunt Olive came into the kitchen.

"I couldn't help overhearing," she said. "I'm trained to hear the mating call of the yellow-bellied sapsucker a mile away. I know exactly where you can get that fabric for free."

"You do? Where?" Mickey asked excitedly.

"The curtains in your bedroom. You said you didn't like them anyway. I guess it's okay if you want to cut them up if it's for your homework."

"Oh, Aunt Olive! They would be perfect. Are you sure

you don't mind?" She threw her arms around her aunt and hugged her.

"It's fine. It's fine," Olive squirmed. "I figure if you're brave enough to make some changes, I can too. What do you think of repainting your bedroom orange?"

When presentation day arrived, Mickey carried her dress to FAB in a simple black garment bag.

"Is that it? Is that your design?" South whispered when she spotted her in the hallway. "Did your dad help you with it?"

"No!" Mickey insisted. "I did it myself." Then she remembered who she was supposed to be. "But I always think to myself, 'What would Daddy do?'"

South nodded. "That's really cool."

"What did you make?" Mars asked as she followed Mickey up the stairs to class. "Mine is so boring. I bet yours is something really special."

"I guess," Mickey replied. "I mean, I worked really hard on it."

In the studio, she carefully pinned her dress to her dress

form and checked that there were no crooked seams or dropped stitches. She looked around the room at the pieces her classmates had made. Mars had reshaped a seventies wrap dress into a simple crop top that tied at the waist and fashioned matching hot pants from the rest of the material. South's design was a denim mini made out of an old pair of jeans, and Gabriel had morphed a pair of men's khaki pants ("borrowed" from his dad's closet!) into a military-style jacket with epaulets on the shoulders.

When Mr. Kaye came to her dress form, he pushed his glasses to the tip of his nose and stared. "I'm speechless," he said.

Mickey held her breath. She wasn't sure if that was a good thing or a bad thing till Gabriel gave her a thumbs-up.

"The workmanship is flawless," her teacher continued as he circled around her design. "Extremely avant-garde. I'm reminded of early Alexander McQueen! I've never seen anything like it in any of my classes. I'm eager to hear what your inspiration was."

"It all started with the Pioneers logo," Mickey explained. "It really spoke to me. This was a small band that traveled all over the country in the nineties trying to make a name for themselves. I wanted my dress to reflect movement, so I split the skirt into three pieces—and the yellow color just felt bright, optimistic, and hopeful. Like the band's lead singer, who really believed he could change the face of music."

Mr. Kaye nodded. "It sounds like you did a great deal of research. Excellent work, Kenzie."

Mickey couldn't wait to find JC in the cafeteria and tell him the news.

"What was the verdict?" he asked as she raced over to his table.

"He loved it. He gave me a four plus."

"Are you kidding me?" JC gasped. "No one gets a four plus in Kaye's class. I doubt even Bridget Lee herself would get a four plus. Mickey, you did it!"

Mickey felt like she was walking on air. Nothing could bring her down, not even Jade strolling over to their table.

"I hear FAB has a new fashion star." She smiled sweetly. "Congrats, Kenzie."

"Um, thanks," Mickey said. "That's really nice of you, Jade."

"Of course it is!" Jade smiled brightly.

"I guess FAB has a new fashion diva, and it's not La Lee," JC teased her.

The smile vanished from Jade's face. "What do you mean?"

"I just mean that Mickey is giving you a run for your money," he replied. "I wouldn't be surprised if she won Runway Showdown this semester."

Jade gritted her teeth. "I'm going to win Showdown," she said.

"Ya think?" JC mocked her. "I wouldn't be too sure about that."

Jade turned to Mickey. "Let's be clear: there's only room for one design diva here, and that's me. You got lucky this time—thanks to me taking you shopping. You're welcome!"

She turned on her wedge heel and strutted back to her table of minions.

"She's delusional," JC said. Then he noticed Mickey's worried look. "You okay?"

Mickey shook off Jade's nasty dig and tried to remind herself that she *had* won this fashion challenge all by herself and wowed her teacher. Her design was great, and no one could take that away from her.

"I'm more than okay," she said. "I'm just getting started."

Easy as ABC

"Earth to Mickey? Come in, Mickey!" her mom said, waving a plate of chocolate chip waffles under her nose. She placed a tall glass of chocolate milk next to it. "It's not like you to let your favorite breakfast get cold."

Mickey sighed. "Sorry, Mom. I was just thinking."

Her mother pulled up a chair at the kitchen table next to her. "Okay. Spill. What's bugging you?"

Mickey didn't know where to begin. When she came home this weekend to Philly, all she could think about was her Apparel Arts final challenge. Mr. Kaye was going to reveal the theme on Monday, and she'd have only a month to design and construct it.

"I just really want to show everyone I belong at FAB," she said quietly.

"Of course you belong!" her mother insisted. "You've

been getting straight As in all of your classes. I couldn't be prouder!"

Mickey nodded. When she told her mom about the four plus on her fashion design, she left out the part about her masquerading as "Kenzie Wills" to win everyone over. What would her mom say if she knew that she was lying every day?

"I know what would cheer you up! Let's hit the flea market," her mom said, sipping her coffee.

Mickey nodded. "I could use a few new outfits for school," she said. "Maybe some cashmere sweaters…"

Her mom nearly spit out her coffee. "Cashmere sweaters? Since when do you like cashmere sweaters? Your taste has certainly changed since you started at that school. What happened to the girl who made her own patchwork pants out of some old tablecloths?"

"I'm just trying to fit in," Mickey insisted. "You should see how Jade dresses! Everything has a designer label."

Her mom looked concerned. "You never used to care what other people wore," she reminded her. "Don't you always tell me, 'I gotta be me'?"

Mickey wished she knew where that girl had gone. The only time she could truly be herself was when she designed for class. As long as she looked and acted like Kenzie Wills, no one laughed or made fun of her when she turned an old rock T-shirt into a couture gown. Kenzie could do anything! Mickey, on the other hand, was a walking fashion disaster.

"I'm still me," she said, taking a bite of waffle. "I just want to save the creativity for my designs."

"Fine," her mom said. "As long as you don't let Jade or anyone else change you." She wiped a smudge of chocolate off Mickey's mouth with a napkin. "I love you just the way you are."

Back at school on Monday, Mickey shifted nervously in her seat as Mr. Kaye took a stack of papers out of his briefcase. "This is your last challenge," he said. "Give it one hundred and ten percent—your grade is depending on it. The top students in each of the three grades will present collections at the Runway Showdown."

Mickey read the sheet carefully:

Style should be as simple as A-B-C. Use these three letters to inspire an alphabetical outfit!

Mars's hand went up immediately. "I don't get it. Are we supposed to use letters in our design?"

"You could," Mr. Kaye replied. "It's open to interpretation."

Mickey's mind began racing. What could she use that started with those three letters?

Mr. Kaye wrote the number twenty on the SMART Board. "This is your budget," he said. "No more than twenty dollars, and I want to see receipts this time, Miss East."

South blushed. "Okay, maybe I did spend an itsy-bitsy bit more on the yard of vicuña for the last challenge…"

"Stick to your budget and stick to your voice as a designer," Mr. Kaye warned. "Wow me!"

Birds of a Feather

Mickey sat with a huge dictionary on her lap, racking her brain for inspiration. "Aardvark, air conditioner, anchovy…" she read aloud. None of them sounded appealing or made any sense for a fashion design.

"Your cauliflower casserole is on the table," Aunt Olive called from the kitchen.

Mickey ignored her and kept flipping pages. Olive poked her head inside the bedroom doorway. "I'm glad you're studying so hard, but you need to take a break. Dinner is ready," she said.

"I'm not studying," Mickey groaned. "I'm trying to break my designer's block."

Olive sat on the edge of the bed. "What are you stumped on? I'm very good at the Sunday crossword puzzle. Maybe I can help."

Mickey closed the dictionary and rested her chin in her hands. "I need to come up with a design that uses three things beginning with the letters *A-B-C*," she explained. "I really wanted to do a jumpsuit in black and white—something graphic."

Olive scratched her head. "By graphic, do you mean you want it to have pictures on it?"

Mickey shrugged. "I guess. Something I could make a pattern out of."

Olive nodded. "I think I have something that would work for your A-B-C theme…"

She went into her room and dug out a large box of photographs. "Let me see. Oh, yes. Here's one." She handed Mickey a photo of a small gray-and-white bird. "American pipit. He was quite a character. Likes to bob his head back and forth. That could be your *A*." She rummaged through the box until she found the other birds she was looking for: "*B* is for blackbird and *C* is for cactus wren."

Mickey looked through the photos—they were nice, but what did birds have to do with fashion? Then an idea struck her like lightning: "I could screen these bird images on white silk, create palazzo pants and an asymmetrical shoulder…"

"I don't know what you're saying, but if your designer's block is broken, can we eat supper?" Olive asked.

"I'm saying you're brilliant, Aunt Olive!" Mickey said, hugging her.

"I am?" Olive replied, slightly flustered. "I mean, I am!"

The day of the presentation, all of FAB was buzzing with excitement. Mickey carried her design in a garment bag over her arm and couldn't wait to unveil it.

"Coming through! Coming through!" Jade shouted, pushing past her as Tinsley the assistant rolled a small clothing rack behind her. "You!" she barked at Gabriel. "Help Tinsley lift it up the stairs."

Gabriel obeyed, and Jade rewarded him by shoving him out of the way. Mickey had no doubt that Jade's design was going to be over-the-top—especially if it required a clothing rack to carry it in!

"What do you think of my design?" JC snuck up behind her. He was wearing a vest made out of CDs.

"I thought your name was JC, not CD," Mickey teased.

JC grinned. "I was going for a knight in shining armor

look—either that or the Tin Man from *The Wizard of Oz*. Do you like my ABCs?"

He twirled around so Mickey could read each of the CD labels. "Pop stars?" she asked.

"Pop *divas*. Ariana, Britney, and Cher," JC replied. "Aaliyah, Beyoncé, and Carey, Mariah. Cool, huh? Bogart was getting rid of his collection, so I got the idea to string them together with fishing line."

"It's amazing," Mickey said admiringly.

"It's hideous," Jake said, walking by them with his garment bag. "That pile of plastic is never going to make it to Runway Showdown."

"Really? What did your mommy make for your presentation?" JC tossed back. "Because we all know that you and Jade never do anything by yourselves."

Mickey elbowed him. "Don't bother, JC. Like Mr. Kaye always says, 'Let the design speak for itself.'"

"And my design is saying, 'I'm so much better than either of yours!'" Jake laughed as he skipped up the steps.

Mickey hoped he wasn't right. She had to make it to the top three. She just had to.

The Big Reveal

As Mickey unzipped her garment bag, the students in her class all elbowed each other to get a first look.

"Let me see!" Mars insisted when Gabriel pushed in front of her.

"Stand back, give the princess some air," he said. "Go ahead, Kenzie."

"You are such a suck-up," South told him. "As if Kenzie wants to give you the time of day."

Mickey didn't know what to say! She'd never had anyone fight to be her friend before, and she surmised it had nothing to do with her and all to do with her lies.

Luckily, Mr. Kaye walked in before a brawl broke out. "Roll your dress forms to the front of the room and line them up," he instructed. "Let's see how they stack up next to each other."

Mars had chosen her ABCs from the world of gemstones: "Amethyst, bloodstone, and coral," she explained. "I recycled some of my personal jewelry collection to create a cocktail dress that shines."

Mr. Kaye jotted down some notes. "It's an interesting take on the little black dress, but I'm not crazy about the fabric you chose," he said. "It's a bit heavy for evening."

"I tried silk," Mars explained. "But the gems were too big and heavy and kept ripping it. So I had to use flannel."

"Flannel is for pajamas and lumberjacks," their teacher snapped. "Next!"

Gabriel's design was a purple hooded cape that draped to the floor.

"I don't understand," Mr. Kaye said. "Where is your ABC theme?"

"Don't you get it?" Gabriel said, chuckling. "I made 'a big cape'!"

Mr. Kaye groaned. "Next!"

South was especially proud of her design—she'd airbrushed graffiti words on a white denim jacket. They read "Artistic. Bold. Cool."

"You're quite a graffiti artist," Mr. Kaye remarked. She beamed. "But I'm not quite sure you're a designer just yet."

When he came to Mickey's design, he circled around it once, then twice, then a third time. She'd accessorized the bird print jumpsuit with a white feathered boa.

"It's striking," he commented after she explained each of the birds' names and how she silkscreened each one onto the fabric in delicate detail. "And the line of the pants is perfection. Palazzo pants can be very tricky, but yours are just the right balance of sleek and billowy."

Mickey smiled. So far, so good. "My only critique is the boa. A bit much, don't you think? I get the feather reference, but it overpowers your jumpsuit. A good designer knows when less is more."

Mickey winced. There went her four plus. But everyone's design had some flaws as well. She hoped she'd scored high enough to make the final cut.

"We will be announcing the top three students for Runway Showdown at two o'clock over the loudspeaker," he told the class when he was finished inspecting their work. "If your name is called, please report to my office for instructions. If it isn't, back to the drawing board and better luck next semester."

As she sat in math class, Mickey stared at the clock on the wall waiting for it to reach two p.m. She knew there was a ton of competition in each of the three grades. JC told her that Mr. Kaye oohed and aahed over Jade's design: a pink cropped angora sweater with a Battenberg lace collar and a white chiffon floor-length skirt.

"It was luxe to the max," he said. "I could totally see it on the runway."

At two sharp, a voice boomed over the loudspeaker. "Ladies and gentleman, may I have your attention," Mr. Kaye said. "I have the names of the three finalists who will be competing in the FAB Runway Showdown this semester."

Mickey held her breath. "In eighth grade, Charlie Hirsch; in seventh grade, Jade Lee; and in sixth grade, Kenzie Wills!"

"Good for you, Kenzie!" her algebra teacher Ms. Rothstein cheered.

Mickey raced to Mr. Kaye's office, where Jade and Charlie were already waiting. Jade gave Mickey a dirty look as she took a seat beside her.

"Congratulations on coming this far," Mr. Kaye said. "Now the real work is ahead of you."

Mickey gulped. What had she gotten herself into?

"You will create a capsule collection consisting of four distinct looks," he continued. "The collection should be a reflection of who you are as a designer—the real you. That said, it must be cohesive, and it must be wearable."

Mickey's mind was racing! An entire collection? Where would she get the money to buy that many materials? She doubted Aunt Olive had another pair of old curtains she'd let her cut up!

Mr. Kaye seemed to read her mind: "The school will provide you with a fabric budget of two hundred and fifty dollars at 'TUDE Fabric. Be smart with how you spend it and feel free to recycle any scraps or materials you already have. Are there any questions?"

"It sounds like a lot for one person," Mickey said softly.

"It is way too much for one person," her teacher agreed with her. "Which is why we are allowing each of you to choose one fellow FAB student to assist you."

"I choose my brother Jake," Jade said.

"I want Dylan Ruff," Charlie said.

"Of course you do," Jade protested. "He won Showdown last spring."

"That leaves you, Kenzie," Mr. Kaye said. "Who do you choose?" Mickey didn't even have to think about it. There was only person at FAB who had been on her side since day one. "JC. I choose JC," she said.

"Hah! The doggie duds dude!" Charlie snickered.

Mr. Kaye hushed them and continued. "After you've created each look, you will fit it on a model, style it, and send it down the runway in front of an audience."

"How will we be judged?" Mickey asked. "What are you looking for?"

"Skill and style," Mr. Kaye said simply. "And of course creativity, originality, and fashion flair. But it won't be just me judging you this time. There will be three other surprise celebrity judges joining me, and you can invite all your family and friends to come to the show."

"My mom will be so excited," Jade cooed. "I bet she'll tweet about it!"

"What about our models?" Charlie asked. "Where do we get them?"

"You can pick four of your friends to walk the runway in your designs. Again, choose wisely."

Mickey was just trying to take it all in—it felt over-whelming and thrilling at the same time. She had no idea what to design for her collection or who she would pick to walk the runway for her. It was so many decisions to make in such a short amount of time!

"You have one month to put it together," Mr. Kaye added finally.

One month! Mickey felt the room starting to spin. How could she do this all in just four short weeks?

"I suggest you start planning immediately—the clock starts now," Mr. Kaye said, dismissing them. "Next stop, Showdown!"

I Gotta Be Me

"So what are you gonna sew?" Annabelle asked, pouring hot fudge on top of a cup of strawberry froyo. "Do you have any ideas?"

Mickey shook her head. "JC and I've been brainstorming for days, but I can't come up with anything good enough. Nothing that reflects the real me. Everything I think of feels boring or wrong."

They sat down at a table and dug into their sundaes. "Do you think maybe you're thinking too much?" her friend suggested. "I mean, when I do a dance routine and all I focus on is the steps, I usually mess it up. Sometimes you have to just let your mind go blank and feel the beat. You know what I'm saying?"

"Kinda," Mickey said. "You think I should just let it come to me."

"Exactly!" Annabelle replied. "Close your eyes and try and picture your designs walking down the runway."

Mickey did as her friend suggested, but all she could see was a parade of models wearing cabbages on their heads! "It's not working. I have no idea who the real me is anymore."

"You look a little different, but you're still the same old Mickey," Annabelle reminded her. "Who else puts cookie dough bites, yogurt chips, marshmallow fluff, peanut butter, and Fruity Pebbles on their froyo? Eww!"

Her mom wasn't much help either. "Why don't you do a collection of animal prints," she said, as they strolled the rows of vendors at the Sunday flea market. She held up a zebra-print scarf. "How about this for inspiration?"

"Pass," Mickey said. "It has to be more special than that."

"Oh, this is *so* you!" her mom teased her, picking out a leopard faux-fur hat and plunking it on Mickey's head. Mickey laughed but quickly went back to feeling anxious over her looming deadline.

Back in NYC, no matter how many fashion magazines she flipped through, her ideas felt flat and uninspired. She ripped page after page out of her sketchbook, crumpled them into a ball, and tossed them over her shoulder.

"What happened in here?" Aunt Olive asked, noticing a mountain of scrap papers littering the floor. "Designer's block again?"

"Not just a block," Mickey replied, frustrated. "A whole wall! All my ideas are awful!"

Olive crossed her hands over her chest. "You don't say. That bad?"

"Worse than bad," Mickey told her. "They're going to kick me out of FAB for being a failure." She felt tears stinging the corners of her eyes and tried to hold them back.

"Did I show you my new briefcase for work?" Olive asked out of the blue.

"Your briefcase?" Mickey asked, wiping her eyes with the back of her hand.

Olive went to the living room and returned with a bright purple leather tote with gold studs around the seams. "Do you like it?" she asked.

Mickey nodded. "It's great—very Valentino Rockstud. But it's not something you'd usually go for."

"Well, that's the thing," Olive said, tossing it over her shoulder. "A very smart, young fashion designer taught me a thing or two about accessorizing. I think I could dial it up a notch every now and then."

Mickey smiled. "Really? I inspired you?"

Olive squeezed her hand and smiled. "You did. I might even consider putting purple streaks in my hair on the weekends…"

Mickey decided it was time to stop moping and start moving. She headed straight to Mr. Kaye's office Monday morning to get his advice.

"I can't tell you what to do," he said sternly. "It has to come from inside you, Kenzie."

Mickey winced when he called her by her "fake" name.

"It's really Mickey," she corrected him. "I know I told you and everyone else to call me Kenzie, but it's not who I am."

"I know," Mr. Kaye replied. "And I think that's your problem. You're pretending to be someone you're not, and it's holding you back."

Mickey thought about what he was saying. But when she started at FAB, no one liked her or gave her the time of day when she was plain old Mickey Williams from Philly. Still, she'd been lying to her teacher—and she wasn't sure how he would take that. What if he was angry with her? What if he reported her to the principal and they revoked her scholarship?

"Is there something you'd like to tell me?" Mr. Kaye prodded her.

"My dad really isn't a Finnish fashion designer," she confided. Then the truth came pouring out: "He's not rich and famous and neither am I. I've never met a king or queen before or even been to Finland once!"

"You don't say." Mr. Kaye tried not to smile. "And do you think any of that matters? Goodness, Coco Chanel started out as a clerk in a hosiery store!"

Mickey looked confused. "You're saying I should sell pantyhose?"

"I'm saying to *own* who you are. Be proud of it. Let Kenzie Wills the designer's collection be a reflection of Mickey Williams the person, inside and out."

Just then Mickey remembered what she wrote on her application essay for FAB: *I want to be a designer who always colors outside the lines and thinks outside of the box...*

"That's it!" she suddenly shouted, leaping out of her chair. "I think I know what I'm going to do for my collection."

Mr. Kaye winked. "I knew you would figure it out sooner or later."

"Thanks so much," she told her teacher. "I've gotta find JC and get started right away!"

JC wasn't sure what to make of the design Mickey had draped over Edith. He circled around the dress form, studying it and scratching his head.

"It looks like crayon scribbles," he said.

"Bingo!" Mickey shouted. "It is crayon—fabric crayon to be exact—that I found at 'TUDE. I used this really cool technique where you draw on the cotton, then you use a hot iron to set it…"

"You lost me. What's the theme of your collection? Kindergarten?"

"No." Mickey laughed. "Outside of the box. I want to color outside of the lines on the fabric so it's one of a kind, and then I want the collection to be literally outside of the box."

"And how are you going to do that?" JC asked.

"I haven't figured that part out yet—but I've got some patterns cut and ready to be sewn. Will you help me?"

They each took a part of the dress—Mickey the bodice and JC the skirt—and sewed it together. Mickey marveled at how perfect JC's stitches were and how his hem was effortlessly straight.

"You are really good," she said. "You don't ever stress, do you?"

JC smiled. "My grandma taught me how to sew," he explained. "She said you just let your hands dance across the fabric—never pull too tight. That's how I do it. And you…" JC admired the elegant draping Mickey was doing on Edith. "You have a real eye for silhouette. I would never have thought to shape the shoulders that way with neoprene. It's fierce."

"I think we make a great team," Mickey said.

JC nodded. "Team Mickey all the way."

Seeing Double

Mickey wanted her collection to be a huge surprise—she didn't even tell JC who would be modeling her designs and handled all the fittings herself.

"You know I'm great at keeping secrets," he protested. "Can't you give me a little hint?"

But Mickey stood her ground. "You've been a great friend and a great help, JC," she said. "I want this to be a surprise for you too. Besides, I need you cheering for me in the front row."

"Fine," JC agreed. "I can do that."

The night before the big Runway Showdown, Mickey couldn't sleep a wink. She was too busy going over every detail of the collection in her head, from the accessories, hair, and makeup, to the music that would be playing in the background. Had she made the right choices? Was her work perfect enough? She felt like this was all a dream. Hadn't it been just a few short years ago she was designing clothes for her dolls? Now she was a *real* designer, proving to her peers and her teachers that she had what it took. It might have been a small step in her fashion career—she hoped there'd be many more runway shows to come—but it felt enormous.

Sporting new pink highlights in her hair, Mickey arrived at FAB, Mr. Kaye was waiting backstage in the auditorium. The runway was draped in a red carpet, and there were lights and speakers hung all over the room. The seats were already filling up as the crowd poured in.

"I am proud of each of you," Mr. Kaye said. "No matter what happens today, no matter who wins, you're all winners in my eyes because you accepted the challenge and you saw it through."

"But there can only be one *true* winner, right?" Jade asked. "I mean, the other two are losers."

Mr. Kaye cleared his throat. "Technically, there is a first, second, and third place that will be decided by myself and the other judges."

He looked over at Mickey, who was nervously checking her watch.

"There's only thirty minutes till the show," he said. "Shouldn't your models be lining up backstage?"

"Or getting their hair and makeup done." Jade pointed to Tinsley, who was frantically trying to style Mars's hair into an updo as she squirmed in her seat.

"Don't worry. I've got it covered." Mickey smiled.

"Are you ready, Charlie?" Mr. Kaye asked, noticing him texting on his phone. "You're up first."

"No sweat," Charlie replied. "Like Kenzie said, I've got it covered."

"Well then, I suppose I should go out there and introduce our panel of esteemed judges." He peeked through the curtains. "It's a full house—standing room only."

Mickey looked and saw JC seated right up front alongside the runway.

"Best of luck," Mr. Kaye said, waving to them as he stepped onstage and left them to their last-minute details.

"Did he say full house?" Charlie asked, suddenly nervous. "That auditorium holds four hundred people!"

"Settle down, settle down, everyone," he instructed, and a hush fell over the crowd. "Welcome to the midterm Runway Showdown featuring FAB's best and brightest design students. I'm sure you're all breathless with anticipation to see what they've come up with. I know our judges are." He motioned to three individuals seated on stools at the end of the runway, facing the stage.

"No way!" Jade said, shoving Mickey and Charlie aside to get a better view of the judging panel. "Do you know who that is?" She pointed to a tall, blond woman dressed in a slinky, black dress and dark sunglasses. "That's Misty Binkley, the supermodel! My mom designed all of her wedding gowns!"

"*All of* her wedding gowns?" Charlie asked. "How many times has she been married?"

"A couple," Jade replied. "I lost count. But she's a fashion icon—and even more important, she loves my mom!"

Mickey rolled her eyes. The show hadn't even started, and Jade already had an advantage.

"Who's the guy with the curly hair and bow tie?" Charlie asked.

Mickey squinted. "Oh, my gosh! That's Mack Rosen!" she said. "He dresses anyone who's anyone in Hollywood. And he's a FAB alum."

"A supermodel and a design legend? Is it getting really stuffy back here or is it me?" Charlie asked, wiping sweat off his brow.

After the crowd was done applauding Misty and Mack, Mr. Kaye held up his hands. "As we all know, the Web has become one of the best ways to chronicle the ever-changing face of fashion. This young lady is one of my favorite fashion bloggers. Please welcome Miss Brittney Zirota!"

Jade squealed. "OMG! I love her! She's the coolest!"

"They're judging us?" Charlie exclaimed. "I'm doomed. I might as well hang up my designs right now and spare myself the embarrassment!"

"I'm sure you did a great job," Mickey tried to reassure him.

"I think there's a closet over there." Jade chuckled. "With lots of hangers."

But it was too late. Mr. Kaye was already announcing his collection.

"First up, please welcome eighth-grader Charlie Hirsch!"

Charlie looked pale. "I think I'm gonna be sick," he whispered to Mickey.

"You can do it," Mickey said, giving him a tiny push out the curtains.

Charlie shook as Mr. Kaye handed him the microphone. "Tell us about your collection, Charlie," he said.

Charlie just stared at all the faces staring back at him. He looked like a deer caught in the headlights.

"What inspired you?" Mr. Kaye pressed him.

"B-b-b-basketball," Charlie stammered, shielding his eyes from the spotlight.

Mr. Kaye waited patiently for him to elaborate. "Anything more you'd like to share with us?"

"B-b-b-basketball," Charlie repeated.

"This is b-b-b-boring," Jade said, yawning. "Can we get this over with so I can show my collection?"

Charlie suddenly took a whistle out of his pocket and blew it. A trio of basketball players bounded out from backstage and began to dribble balls down the runway. Each was dressed in a bold, sporty look—bright-red shorts and a matching striped athletic tank; a royal-blue tee with neon-yellow sweatpants, a purple tracksuit with the number one emblazoned in silver on the back. For the finale, the captain of FAB's basketball team ran down the runway spinning a basketball on both pointer fingers. The balls were painted gold to match his outfit: gold-striped running shorts and a sleeveless black hoodie with gold zipper pockets. Mack Rosen leaped to his feet and gave the collection a standing ovation as Charlie took a bow and raced backstage panting.

"I thought I was gonna faint right there on the

runway," he said, collapsing in a heap on the floor. "That was terrifying!"

"And pretty amazing," Mickey said. "Do you hear those cheers? That's for you, Charlie."

Charlie sat up and listened. "Really? They liked it?"

"They loved it," Mr. Kaye said, finding him backstage. "What a brilliant concept: couture meets the basketball court. Mack Rosen is raving!"

Jade sniffed. "Well, he hasn't seen my collection yet." She snapped her fingers, and Tinsley appeared at her side. "Are the models ready?" she asked.

Tinsley nodded. "Check!"

Before Mr. Kaye could even go back out to introduce her, Jade grabbed the microphone and strutted down the runway.

"Hello, everyone! I'm Jade Lee, and my collection is all about style in sync! I would also like to point out that although I love haute couture, I understand the needs of tweens to look fashionable on a budget. So no outfit in my collection would retail for more than twenty-five dollars."

Mickey frowned. "What does she know about shopping on a budget?" she said, bristling. "She has her own gold card!"

"It's a smart strategy." Charlie sighed. "Mr. Kaye will

love it and so will the audience." The crowd was already oohing and aahing in anticipation.

Jade was eating it up. "Without further ado, I give you #twinning by Jade Lee House of Style!"

"She has a house of style?" Charlie asked. "Since when?"

The lights dimmed, and the music began to pulse. First out on the runway were South and Jake in coordinating red outfits. South's had a red chiffon high-low skirt and a fitted white tank topped with a crochet lace vest. Jake wore a red satin blazer over a white tee and jeans.

Next on the runway were Mars and Gabriel in matching black pleather moto jackets. Hers was paired with a red satin romper, while his was worn over a black tee and black jeans with red satin cuffs.

For the finale, Jade appeared onstage pushing a full-length mirror on wheels beside her.

"Oh no," Mickey said. "One Jade was bad enough. Now there's two of her!"

"She did another look? Five?" Charlie gasped. "I could barely finish my four!"

Jade twirled around in a red satin trench coat. She blew kisses to her image in the mirror, then opened the coat to reveal a black satin minidress covered in red sequin hearts and "XOs." The crowd went wild.

"What do you call that look? I love me? I really, really love me?" Charlie said, groaning.

"Stunning!" Misty cheered. "I must have that dress!"

Mickey felt a tap on her shoulder backstage. It was Bogart, and he had her secret weapon unloaded from the trunk of the limo with him.

"You ready?" he asked her. "Everything's all set up."

Mickey took a deep breath. "Ready as I'll ever be."

Out of the Box

Mr. Kaye glanced back to make sure she was ready. When Mickey nodded, he announced into the microphone, "Ladies and gentleman, I would like to present our sixth-grade finalist Miss Kenzie Wills!"

JC whistled through his teeth. "Go, Mickey!" he shouted as she stepped onto the runway to introduce her capsule collection.

"When I think about fashion, I think about something that makes a statement," Mickey explained, stepping up to the microphone. "Something that tells people who you are, where you come from, and where you're going. The inspiration for my collection is 'Out of the Box' because that's how I design. I don't think you should ever let anything or anyone hold you back. In fact, I've decided to call my fashion label 'ME by Kenzie Wills,' not just because those are the initials of my name, Mackenzie Elizabeth, but because it represents who I really am. Hope you like it!"

The lights dimmed, and Bogart rolled a large, white, wooden box on the stage. Mickey stepped forward and opened the door of the box, just as the music began booming over the speakers. Out stepped her mom wearing a kimono-style dress made of the scribble print fabric Mickey had created. As she reached the end of the runway, a blue spotlight hit the fabric, and the print glowed in the dark.

"Whoa!" JC exclaimed. "Didn't see that coming!"

The next time Mickey opened the door to the box, it was Annabelle's turn to strut out onstage. She was wearing a dance costume Mickey had designed for her: a one-shouldered crop top and bootie shorts with long floor-length fringe attached at the waist. Annabelle pirouetted around the stage, and the fringe danced around her.

Next up out of the box was Aunt Olive! Her look was a stylish suit jacket with pointy padded shoulders and a nipped-in waist over a short pencil skirt. Both were made from the scribble print, and to go with it, Mickey had designed her a bright-yellow feather fascinator hat. She had never seen her aunt smile so much. At the end of the runway, she even struck a pose and winked at the judges!

All of a sudden, the music stopped abruptly and the auditorium went dark.

Mr. Kaye tried to calm the audience. "Everyone please stay in your seats. There must be a power surge."

But it was all part of Mickey's plan. In a few minutes—just long enough for her to get changed and duck inside the white box—Bogart flipped the lights and music back on. She kicked the door of the box open and twirled out on the stage in a pale-blue strapless ball gown and Dr. Martens. Her hair was streaked with rainbow-colored chalk highlights, and when she spun around, a cloud of rainbow tulle peeked out from under her skirt. Beside her, prancing on a Swarovski-crystal-studded leash, was Madonna the Chihuahua, dressed in a tiara and one of JC's canine couture designs. JC was so surprised he almost fell off his seat. Everyone in the auditorium applauded wildly.

"Brava! Brava!" Mr. Kaye congratulated Mickey as she took her bows. "I knew you could do it. Where did you get the idea for this avant-garde ball gown?"

"Well, I always did love giving princess dolls a make-over," she admitted. "This was my spin on Cinderella."

She noticed that Brittney Zirota was frantically taking

notes and snapping pics on her phone. She hoped that was a good thing!

When she got backstage, Jade was standing with her arms crossed over her chest.

"That was *interesting*," Jade told her. "Certainly not my taste. But interesting."

"It was awesome!" Charlie said, hugging Mickey. "Especially the blackout fake-out part!"

Mickey smiled. She'd done her very best, and now all that was left to do was wait for the judges to deliberate.

When Mr. Kaye returned to the stage fifteen minutes later, he had an envelope in his hand. "May I have all three of our finalists onstage," he asked. "I have the judges' decision."

Mickey, Jade, and Charlie all took their places beside their teacher. Mickey held her breath as he opened the envelope and pulled out the results.

"In third place, Charlie Hirsch!" he read, patting Charlie on the back. "I do believe Mack Rosen wants to discuss you interning with him over the holiday break," he whispered in his ear. "Good job!"

Mickey's heart was pounding. That meant either she or Jade was the winner.

"In second place—" Mr. Kaye read—"congratulations, Kenzie Wills!"

Mickey's heart sank, and her teacher saw the disappointment in her eyes. "There's always next time," he whispered in her ear.

"And I am proud to present the winner of the FAB fall semester Runway Showdown, Jade Lee!" Jade practically grabbed the gold trophy out of his hands.

"I did it! I won!" she yelled to the crowd. "Yay, me!"

Mr. Kaye found Mickey backstage where her friends and family were consoling her. "I couldn't be prouder of you," he said.

"We're so proud of you too," her mom added. Annabelle and Olive nodded in agreement. "Everything you designed was beautiful."

"Thanks." Mickey tried her best to be a good sport, but it hurt to see Jade onstage waving the cup over her head and blowing kisses to the judges. It didn't seem fair, not when she had poured her heart and soul into her collection!

"Don't worry, Mickey," Annabelle said. "Those judges have no taste in fashion!"

"I'm wearing my suit to work on Monday." Olive tried to cheer her up. "Even the hat! I'm a changed woman."

"Thanks," Mickey said. "I know you can't win 'em all, but it would have been nice…."

"Well, maybe this will cheer you up," said a voice behind her. It was Brittany Sirota, and she had made her way backstage to congratulate the finalists.

"I loved your collection, and I want to feature it and you on my fashion blog," she said. "Would that be cool with you?"

Mickey's eyes lit up. "Cool? It would be the most amazing thing that's ever happened to me!"

"I think you're a fashion force to be reckoned with, Kenzie Wills," Brittany added.

"That's my brand name," she corrected her. "Maybe you could just call me Mickey?"

Brittany smiled. "Sure. If you call me Clementine. I was named after my great-granny. Brittany's really my middle name."

Mickey giggled. "Okay, Clementine, it's a deal!"

A New Attitude

After the Runway Showdown, Mickey had two weeks to be home in Philly for the holidays. It felt both wonderful and strange to be back in her old apartment again, but she was looking forward to spending time with her mom and Annabelle.

Her mom brought her breakfast in bed, and they snuggled under the covers.

"I took the whole week off so we could hang out," she told Mickey. "I know life here is probably not as exciting as New York City…"

"No," Mickey said. "It's perfect. I love being home with you for the holidays. I just kind of feel bad leaving Aunt Olive all alone."

"Yeah?" her mom asked. "Then I guess it's a good thing I invited her to spend Christmas Eve with us."

"You did?" Mickey asked excitedly. "You're getting along?"

"Well, we're trying," her mom replied. "I told her she couldn't bring her parakeet, and that didn't go over very well…"

Mickey laughed. "She'll get over it."

Annabelle invited her over to help trim the tree and bake cookies.

"I've never seen a gingerbread man wearing a leather jacket and red high tops," Annabelle commented, watching Mickey pipe frosting on her cookie. "You are definitely one of a kind!"

When it came time to go back to FAB, Mickey decided she should stop worrying what Jade or anyone else thought of her and dress the way she wanted. She chose a pair of purple paisley leggings and a black sweater and clipped a purple feather into her hair. As she as boarded the bus to FAB, all the students applauded her as she took her seat.

"Your collection was so cool," a seventh-grader leaned over to tell her. "Way cooler than Jade's. You should have won Showdown."

126

"Thanks," Mickey said, blushing.

"Kenzie! Kenzie! Kenzie!" the boys in the backseat who had once pelted her with a banana peel were chanting.

Mickey watched out the window but couldn't help smiling. She felt positively famous—and not for being some faux Finnish socialite. For being true to herself and her designs.

JC was waiting for her when she got to her locker.

"Happy New Year! How does it feel to be a FAB celebrity?" he asked.

"Good," she said. "Okay, great."

"You know you'll win next time, right?" he said. "Jade's just a fashion fad. But you're going to be a design legend one day."

"You really think so?" Mickey asked.

Madonna barked her approval from inside his bag.

"Madonna's never wrong about fashion," JC insisted. "When Dom won season twelve of *Project Runway*, she totally called it."

Mickey laughed. "Well, I wouldn't want to argue with Madonna—or you," she said. "But I'm late for Apparel Arts. Mr. Kaye will kill me. See you at lunch?"

JC grinned. "I'll save you a seat, but I might have to fight off all your FAB fans."

Mr. Kaye arrived seconds after she took her seat and wrote the number one on the board. Gabriel groaned. "There he goes again," he whispered to her. "Think you could help me with the next assignment? I can't fail this class again. No one deserves that much torture!"

Mickey chuckled. "Sure. I'd be happy to."

"Welcome back," their teacher announced. "You've survived the first semester, and now it's back to the drawing board—literally. Who's up for challenge number one?"

Mickey got out her notebook and got ready to take notes—then she noticed Mr. Kaye standing over her table. He held out a small, plastic rhinestone wand in his hand.

"This challenge is called Fashion Fairy Godmother," he said. "I'd like to see how each of you reinterprets a fairy-tale princess like Sleeping Beauty or Cinderella. Kenzie will be the judge."

"Me?" Mickey gasped. "I get to judge everybody's work?"

"Just this one time," he said with a wink. "Unless, of course, you win the next Showdown."

Mickey couldn't way for her next chance to rock the runway. The possibilities were endless...

Carrie's Style File: Meet Designer Zara Terez!

Zara happens to be one of my fave fashion designers—not only do I wear her skirts, leggings, and bags, but I have her giant cookie print blanket on my bed! She's known for her cool photo prints (stuff like doughnuts, paper clips, even SoulCycle bikes!) and bold colors, and was nice enough to tell me all about her line and her inspiration.

Carrie: How do you find out about the latest fashion trends?

Zara: We take a lot of inspiration from the streets of New York City, where we design, manufacture, and produce all of our garments. We know what we like and what makes up happy, and we stick to that—which usually means any and all types of food, color, and glitter!

Carrie: How do you get your ideas for your designs? Does anyone or anything in particular inspire you?

Zara: I get to design everything with my best friend from childhood, and it's like we share a brain. A rainbow/glitter/cupcake brain that is always churning with new ideas. We remind each other every day of the things that made us happy as kids and what continues to excite us as, well, bigger kids! The beauty of what I do is that there are no limits and the possibilities are endless. There are no rules in our world. That makes it really easy to come up with fun, new, exciting designs every day. Being able to always live outside the box.

Carrie: What makes "Zara Terez" different from any other clothing line?

Zara: *Everything!* We are not just another clothing line. We consider the Zara Terez brand to be a lifestyle. We encourage freedom of expression through fashion, individuality, and positive living. We are 100 percent made in the USA, and a big focus of ours is *quality*. We want to provide our customers with a product we are proud of and a product they feel amazing in. Nothing is more important than feeling good about yourself.

Carrie: What advice do you have for children who want to become fashion designers when they grow up?

Zara: You go for it! Reach for the stars. Never doubt yourself. The sky is the limit. Anything is possible.

Carrie: What is your favorite part about being a fashion designer?

Zara: Getting to see my designs walk down the street! It's incredible to know that they chose my design over anyone else's that day and that the garment I worked so hard to create is how they have chosen to represent themselves in that moment.

Carrie: What have you learned from being a fashion designer?

Zara: Making mistakes is okay as long as you learn from them. No one is perfect, and things aren't always going to run smoothly, especially in a business like ours. But by keeping an open mind, working your butt off, and making sure you stay organized, focused, positive, and true to yourself, anything in the world can be done.

Acknowledgments

Many thanks to all our friends and family:

Daddy/Peter: you always make us smile—especially with your crazy party shirts!

The Kahns, Berks, and Saps: love you to the moon and back!

Kyle Rothstein: Now a Bar Mitzvah! We're so proud of you!

Lizz Errico: Carrie came up with the idea for this book in your fifth-grade class at PS6! Hope you love it as much as we do.

Ally Lax, Annabelle Haroche, Gaby Hirsch: hope you like seeing your names in print ;-)

Ms. Archer, Carrie's English teacher at TDS: thanks for teaching her this year and helping her make her writing shine.

A big thanks to the fashionably fabulous Zara Terez for her interview and to Stephanie Goldstein of Stoopher and Boots (our fave store for cool clothes!) for introducing us!

The folks at Sourcebooks, especially Steve Geck, Kate Prosswimmer, Alex Yeadon, and Elizabeth Boyer. We love how enthusiastic you always are about our ideas! Love working with you all.

Katherine Latshaw and Frank Weimann at Folio Lit: thanks for all your hard work and support.

Here's a sneak peek at the next
book in the Fashion Academy series!

Fashion Academy: Runway Ready

Mr. Kaye was quite the master at inventing original—and perplexing—fashion design challenges for his students. Mickey had come to accept that she would never know what to expect when he walked through the studio door and drew a number on the SMART Board. Today, it was the number three.

"Clients can be extremely difficult," he began. "And part of becoming a successful designer is learning how to interpret what they want and give it to them."

Gabriel gulped. "I don't have a good feeling about this," he whispered to Mickey.

"I'd like you all to meet your client." A little girl strolled into the room and stood facing the students. She was dressed in an adorable smocked pink dress, white ruffled socks, and shiny black Mary Janes.

"Aww, she's so cute!" Mars cooed. "Hi, ya sweetie!"

The child stuck her tongue out and stomped her foot. "I am not cute. Cute is for babies! And don't call me sweetie! You're a dum-dum!"

The class erupted in laughter. "You tell her, kid!" Gabriel said, applauding.

"You're a dum-dum too!" the tot fired back.

"This is Miss Cordelia Vanderweil," Mr. Kaye said, trying to calm everyone down. "If we could keep the name-calling to a minimum, Cordy, dear?"

"As in Victoria Vanderweil? The famous fashion designer who practically launched the designer jean craze in the seventies?" Mickey gasped.

"The one and only. This young lady is her granddaughter."

Cordelia looked over the crowd of faces staring at her. "Granny Vicky isn't gonna like any of you," she said. "You're all mean and icky!"

South flinched. "I've been called a lot of things before, but never 'icky'!"

"You don't mean that," Mr. Kaye insisted, taking the child's hand. "These lovely students are going to design you a pretty dress for your fifth birthday party." He then turned to face the class. "And Granny Vicky is going to be the judge of who wins this challenge."

"No way!" Mars shouted. "Victoria Vanderweil is going to grade our designs? That is amazing!"

"Well, that depends," Mr. Kaye pointed out. "On how amazing your designs are."

Gabriel raised his hand. "What are the guidelines?"

"You will have to ask Miss Cordelia that," Mr. Kaye replied. "Cordy, they're all yours."

"I want a fancy dress," the child rattled off. "With bows and buttons! Oh, and balloons!"

Gabriel raised an eyebrow. "You want balloons on the dress—or attached to it?"

Cordelia waved her hand dismissively. "I like pink and purple and red and yellow and orange and blue. I like twirly ballerinas. Oh! And the Easter Bunny!"

Mickey scratched her head. This was a tall order to fill! "You mean these are your favorite things you want at your party? Or things you want us to think about when designing your dress?"

"Rainbows! I love rainbows and spaghetti!"

"Do you all think you have enough information?" Mr. Kaye asked the class. "I do believe Cordelia has lunch at the Plaza Hotel with her granny shortly."

"You better do a good job!" she said, leaving them with a stern warning. "Or else!"

"I second that," Mr. Kaye said. "You have one week to complete your challenge. Good luck—you'll need it."

When Mickey got home from school, she pulled out her sketchbook and began drawing. But instead of a party dress design, she found herself doodling a hot air balloon with Cordelia and the Easter Bunny sitting in it. They were eating a bowl of spaghetti and meatballs as the balloon wafted in the clouds.

She decided to call JC. If he could whip up clothes for his Chihuahua Madonna, maybe he'd have some ideas of how to design for a temperamental tot.

"Wow, that's quite a wish list to fill," he said, listening intently as Mickey rattled off all of Cordelia's requirements. "Where does the spaghetti come in?"

"I don't have any idea," Mickey said. "I was thinking a metallic rainbow fabric for the ball gown skirt, tulle underneath that evokes a tutu, and short puffed sleeves that are balloon-like. Then a faux fur stole that looks like a bunny rabbit?"

"Like I said, where does the spaghetti come in?"

Mickey flopped back on her pillow and closed her eyes. "I just don't see how I can work it into the design. It doesn't go. Everything is light and fluffy; spaghetti is long and slippery."

"What about the accessories. Maybe you can put a plate of spaghetti on Cordy's darling little head?" JC suggested.

"You're not helping," Mickey moaned. "This is a huge challenge. Victoria Vanderweil is going to see my design."

"I say ditch the pasta and make her a purse instead."

Suddenly, a lightbulb went off over Mickey's head.

"Say that again!"

"Ditch the pasta?"

"No!" Mickey exclaimed. "The part about making her a purse. How about a purse that has long strands of gold fringe, just like spaghetti? JC, you're a genius!"

"That I am," her friend replied. "That I am."

About the Authors

Sheryl Berk has written about fashion for more than twenty years, first as a contributor to *InStyle* magazine, and later as the founding editor in chief of *Life & Style Weekly*. She has written dozens of books with celebrities including Britney Spears, Jenna Ushkowitz, Whitney Port, and Zendaya—and the #1 *New York Times* bestseller (turned movie) *Soul Surfer* with Bethany Hamilton. Her daughter, Carrie Berk, is a renowned cupcake connoisseur and blogger (www.facebook.com/PLCCupcakeClub; www.carriescupakecritique.shutterfly.com) with over 101K followers at the tender young age of twelve! Carrie is a fountain of fabulous ideas for book series—she came up with Fashion Academy in the fifth grade. Carrie learned to sew from her grandma "Gaga" and has outfitted many an American Girl doll in original fashions. The Berks also write the deliciously popular series The Cupcake Club.

Check out Carrie's new fashion blog:
www.fashionacademybook.com.

Love the book? Get the look! Fashion Academy–inspired shirts available at Purple Pixies:
http://shop.purplepixies.net.

GLITTER GIRL
Toni Runkle and Stephen Webb

Meet Kat Connors of Carmel, Indiana: trendsetter, fashion blogger, and Glitter Girl Cosmetics' newest Alpha Girl. Kat is tapped to try out all of Glitter Girl's hottest beauty products before they hit the stores. Forty-eight hours after she blogs about the goodies in the new line, every girl at her school is sporting the gear. Kat's popularity skyrockets, but Jules—Kat's BFF—seems to be the only one who's not buying into the Glitter Girl lifestyle. Is Kat willing to sacrifice her friendship for life in the fab lane?

PRAISE FOR *GLITTER GIRL*:

"Do you have a passion for fashion and beauty? If so, you might want to add *Glitter Girl* by Toni Runkle and Stephen Webb to your collection of must reads." —*Girls' Life Magazine*

MODEL UNDERCOVER: PARIS

Carina Axelsson

A CRIME OF FASHION

Axelle Andersen wants nothing more than to be a teen sleuth despite the influence of her pushy fashionista Aunt Venetia. So when top fashion designer Belle La Lune goes missing, and Aunt Venetia becomes a prime suspect, Axelle must go undercover as a model during Paris Fashion Week to uncover the truth behind Belle's disappearance and clear her aunt's name. She's thrust into a frenetic world of castings, photo shoots, and sequins, while struggling to fit in and track down clues. Can Axelle solve a kidnapping and survive the world of fashion?

MODEL UNDERCOVER: NEW YORK

Carina Axelsson

STOLEN WITH STYLE

When the world's most famous black diamond is stolen during a magazine cover shoot, it's up to undercover model Axelle Anderson to crack the case. The only witness is a trendsetting teen fashion blogger who refuses to say anything, and Axelle has a hunch that what appears to be a clear-cut case of jewelry theft is anything but.

Axelle and her sleuthing friends are drawn into a web of blackmail and backstabbing fashionistas. As she struts her way down the New York City runways and juggles her busy modeling schedule and new romance, Axelle must pit herself against a rival who'll stop at nothing to bring her down.

THE ALLEGRA BISCOTTI COLLECTION
Olivia Bennett

SHE'S THE HOTTEST NEW FASHION DESIGNER WITH A BIG SECRET!

Emma Rose is SO not a diva.

She doesn't want her turn on the catwalk—she'd rather be behind the scenes creating fabulous outfits! So when a famous fashionista discovers Emma's designs and offers her the opportunity of a lifetime—a feature in *Madison* magazine (squeal!)—Emma sort of, well, panics. She only has one option: to create a secret identity. And so Allegra Biscotti is born.

Allegra is worldly, sophisticated, and bold—everything Emma is not. But the pressure is on. And Emma quickly discovers juggling school, a new crush, friends, and a secret identity might not be as glamorous as she thought.

WHO WHAT WEAR

The Allegra Biscotti Collection

Olivia Bennett

Emma Rose is SO not famous.

So how did she score inside information on the most talked-about party of the year? Because Emma is secretly the hottest new fashion designer—Allegra Biscotti—and hired to whip up a Sweet Sixteen dress for the guest of honor. But how to keep her secret identity, well, a secret? Emma's got one option—go under cover as her own intern!

But Emma's BFF is starting to get suspicious at the same time that Jackson finally starts paying attention to her... Can Emma make it work, or will it all come apart at the seams?

Peace Love and CUPCAKES

Meet Kylie Carson.

She's a fourth grader with a big problem. How will she make friends at her new school? Should she tell her classmates she loves monster movies? Forget it. Play the part of a turnip in the school play? Disaster! Then Kylie comes up with a delicious idea: What if she starts a cupcake club?

Soon Kylie's club is spinning out tasty treats with the help of her fellow bakers and new friends. But when Meredith tries to sabotage the girls' big cupcake party, will it be the end of the cupcake club?

Book
1

Recipe For Trouble

Meet Lexi Poole.

To Lexi, a new school year means back to baking with her BFFs in the cupcake club. But the club president, Kylie, is mixing things up by inviting new members. And Lexi is in for a not-so-sweet surprise when she is cast in the school's production of *Romeo and Juliet*. If only she could be as confident onstage as she is in the kitchen. The icing on the cake: her secret crush is playing Romeo. Sounds like a recipe for trouble!

Can the girls' friendship stand the heat, or will the cupcake club go up in smoke?

Book
2

Winner Bakes All

Meet Sadie.

When she's not mixing it up on the basketball court, she's mixing the perfect batter with her friends in the cupcake club. Sadie's definitely no stranger to competition, but the oven mitts are off when the club is chosen to appear on *Battle of the Bakers*, the ultimate cupcake competition on TV. If the girls want a taste of sweet victory, they'll have to beat the very best bakers. But the real battle happens off camera when the club's baking business starts losing money. Long recipe short, no money for icing and sprinkles means no cupcake club.

With the clock ticking and the cameras rolling, will the club and their cupcakes rise to the occasion?

Book
3

Icing on the Cake

Meet Jenna.

She's the cupcake club's official taste tester, but the past few weeks have not been so sweet. Her mom just got engaged to Leo—who Jenna is sure is not "The One"—and Peace, Love, and Cupcakes has to bake the wedding cake. Jenna is ready to throw in the towel, especially when she hears the wedding will be in Las Vegas on Easter weekend, one of the most important holidays for the club's business!

Can Jenna and her friends handle their busy orders—and the Elvis impersonators—or will they have a cupcake meltdown?

Book
4

Baby Cakes

ℳeet Delaney.

New cupcake club member Delaney is shocked to find out her mom is expecting twins! When her parents first tell her, the practical joker thinks they must be pulling her leg. For ten years she's had her parents—and her room—all to herself. She LIKED being an only child. But now she's going to be a big sis.

The girls of Peace, Love, and Cupcakes get together to bake cupcakes and discover Delaney is worried about what kind of a big sister she will be. She's never even babysat before! But her cupcake club friends rally to her side for a crash course in Big Sister 101.

Book

5

Royal Icing

$\mathcal{M}$eet Kylie.

As the founder and president of Peace, Love, and Cupcakes, Kylie's kept the club going through all kinds of sticky situations. But when PLC's advisor surprises the group with an impromptu trip to London, the rest of the group jumps on board—without even asking Kylie. All of sudden, Kylie's noticing the club doesn't need their president nearly as much as they used to. To top it off, the girls get an order for two thousand cupcakes from Lady Wakefield of Wilshire herself—to be presented in the shape of the London Bridge! Talk about a royal challenge...

Can Kylie figure out her place in the club in time to prevent their London Bridge—and PLC—from falling down?

Book

6

Sugar and Spice

$\mathcal{M}$eet Lexi.

The girls of Peace, Love, and Cupcakes might be sugar and spice and everything nice, but the same can't be said for Meredith, whose favorite hobby is picking on Lexi. So when the PLC gets a cupcake order from the New England Shooting Starz—the beauty pageant Meredith is competing in—the girls have a genius idea: enter Lexi into the competition so she can show Meredith once and for all that she's no better than anyone else. Problem is, PLC has to make Lexi a pageant queen—and 1,000 cupcakes—all in a matter of weeks!

Have the girls of Peace, Love, and Cupcakes bitten off more than they can chew?

Book

7